REVENGE IS SWEET

MAFIA BRIDES

LEE SAVINO

REVENGE IS SWEET

Previously published as "Taken by the Mafia Prince" in the Darkly Ever After Boxset.

***

She's gonna bake him a muffin he can't refuse...

When a mafia prince sweeps into Leah's bakery and decides she belong to him, all's she can do is can hang on until the happily ever after.

DEDICATION

Dedicated to all the curvy girls who are great at baking and deserve love even when we burn the occasional dishcloth.

Also Nanette, who is a cookie and chocolate goddess. You deserve to have your own tall, dark, mafia man steal you away.

A big thank you to Ines Johnson for a fabulous beta and sensitivity read. You deserve all the chocolate!

And special thanks to the Goddess Group, who helped with the poll to choose a fun title. Here are all the titles that got a lot of votes but didn't win:

- *Death & Cupcakes*
- *"Revenge is a dish best served with Chocolate Sprinkles"*
- *"Bullets, Blood & Blonde Brownies"*
- *"Bullets and Buttercream"*
- *"GUNS & SCONESES"*
- *"There's a Chocolate Horse Head in my Bed"*
- *"Say hello to my little... flan"*
- *Keep your Friends close and your Eclairs Closer"*

Join Lee Savino's Goddess Group on Facebook or follow me on Tiktok for more wacky fun.

1

The sun's just waking up as I trudge from the bus stop through piles of matted and dirty snow. On this gray February morning, there's only one shop whose windows are lit up in the dark and rundown strip mall. Even with the scuffed and faded pale pink paint, the bakery is a cheery and welcoming sight.

The door sticks, but when I lean my weight into it, it stutters open and sets the overhead bell jingling merrily. My mouth begins watering a second before the caramel and cinnamon scents hit me in a blast of warmth.

Heaven is a bakery ten minutes before opening. Specifically, Panetteria Principessa, the best bakery in my hometown, Dumont, and possibly all of the world. It doesn't matter that my cheap boots are soggy or that my cheeks are chapped with cold. It's gonna be a good day.

"Good morning," I trill, stomping my feet to shake off the crust of dirty ice. The shop is warm and smells like cinnamon buns. The scent gives me a sugar rush.

"*Buongiorno*, Leah!" Mr. Rossi shouts from the back, glee radiating through his tone. "Come see what I have done!"

"One sec." I turn and yank on the door handle, making the bell dance and ring again and again. "The door is sticking." Cold air leaks through the cracks.

"I will fix it later. You must come and see!"

"You're gonna pay a ton in heating costs," I warn, but I give up tugging and stroll further into the shop.

"I already do." Mr. Rossi sounds cheerful, but I wince. Heating bills suck. It's not like we can keep the front door closed. Every new customer will bring in an unwelcome blast of winter.

It's a good day to bake, if only to keep the oven on.

The front cases are already filled with chocolate muffins and red velvet cupcakes topped with the most perfect pillowy frosting. A few steps past the counter is the doorway to the back. There's no door, and when I step through, I'm embraced by the yeasty scent of cinnamon rolls and the bright citrus scent of lemon poppy seed muffins.

I'm so lucky to work in my favorite place in the world.

To the left are all the ovens, giving off delicious heat. I tug off my thin coat and unwind my cream-colored scarf. Underneath my winter things, I'm wearing a soft pink sweater that makes my brown skin glow. The knit fabric would be too hot to work in if I were back here all day, but as I'm alternating between the front and the back, it will be perfect.

In the corner, Mr. Rossi's head sticks out from a row of huge shiny cylinders sitting on an ornate metal box—some sort of machine I've never seen before.

"Ahh, there she is!" His weathered face splits into a smile. "Descending like an angel from heaven."

I chuckle and shed my matching cream mittens and hat. There's nothing flirtatious about my boss's exuberance. He's a sweetheart to everyone. Besides, he's madly in love with his wife.

"You must come see!" he cries, waving his hands in joy. A thin fringe of dark curls bounces around his otherwise bald pate. Light reflects between both the pale patch of bare skin on the top of his head and the metal antique that dominates the corner of the room. "I have found the answer to all our troubles."

The answer to all our troubles is a metallic monstrosity, sitting on a cart. It's taller than I am, with three cylindrical turrets on the top of a brass box.

"What is it?"

"*Una macchina per caffè espresso.* Very vintage. Very rare. I have finally found it! The machine that will turn beans into gold!"

"This is the espresso machine?" When Mr. Rossi told me he was bidding on one at an auction, I was excited. But I was not expecting this. "How old is it?"

"Thirty, forty years... but it works fine."

Oh God. This thing is older than I am.

Mr. Rossi must not see my expression, because he continues. "Cappuccino, latte, *il caffè*—it makes it all. Soon, we will be printing money!"

I hide my sigh. I've heard this before. I can only hope this time, it's true. "What did Cedella say?"

"She has not seen it yet." His face falls. "Only a picture. She can't do stairs, not today."

Mrs. Rossi—Cedella—has the swollen joints of advanced rheumatoid arthritis. Today must be one of her bad days. The cold makes her body ache so bad, she mostly stays in bed.

"I'll make her favorite scones today," I announce.

"Maybe by then we'll have this working and we can make her a latte—she can be the first to try a cup."

"Yes." He brightens. "Thank you, Leah. You are an angel. Soon, she will be better." He grabs a rag and starts polishing the machine.

"Did you look into the infusion treatments?" I ask. "I hear the results are almost miraculous."

"Yes, yes, just need a bit more money for that. But that is where this comes in..." He gives the machine another swipe. "A little beans, a little water, and we will be printing money!"

"Right." I hate to be the voice of reason, but someone has to be. Mrs. Rossi is usually around to ground her husband after his flights of fancy, but she's stuck upstairs, so it'll have to be me. "Um... does it work?"

"Of course! Just needs a little bit of polish." With a final swipe, Mr. Rossi tosses aside the rag and rubs his hands together. "Good as new. Help me move it, darling girl."

Mr. and Mrs. Rossi took me under their wing and gave me a job when I was fifteen and in foster care. Now, I make enough to live on my own even though money is tight. For them, I would do anything.

It takes both of us to roll the machine out, and by the time we've lifted the heavy monstrosity off the cart and onto a clear section at the very end of the side counter, I'm sweating, and my sweater is smudged with the last bit of dust. I have to admit, the machine looks very fancy.

"*Perfetto*," Mr. Rossi announces. "Now we will be printing money!"

"As soon as we learn to use it," I remind him. "Is there an instruction manual?"

"Not that I know of." Mr. Rossi rubs his head until his curls spring up in a childish halo.

"That's okay," I say. The original manual was probably

written in Chaucer's English. Or an obscure Italian dialect. "I'll figure it out." I pat the machine, and something falls off the back with a clang. I snatch my hand back.

"We will be printing money!" Mr. Rossi dashes to the back and returns with a stack of the white paper cups we use for the drip coffee. He's so excited, he drops a few cups on the floor, and they promptly roll under the counter.

Mr. Rossi scrambles around the counter and crouches in front of the chalkboard sign we use as a menu.

"Um, maybe we should wait until we've figured out how —" I start, but he's already adding the word *Lattes* in a barely legible scrawl underneath the usual list of coffee, tea, and daily muffin flavor.

Guess we're making lattes now.

"Do we have enough milk?" I ask, coming to stand next to him. "Because lattes require milk."

"Oh. No." Mr. Rossi scratches his head.

"All right." I carefully erase what he's written and write out *Espresso* in my neat script. "Let's start small." I frown at the espresso maker. "Are you sure there's no instruction manual? Maybe a Latin scroll, handwritten by monks?"

Mr. Rossi has already disappeared into the back. He comes back out carrying a box filled with several shiny pieces, and lengths of opaque plastic hosing. "I forgot to reattach these," he says and ducks his head like a little boy with his hand caught in the biscotti jar.

The oven buzzer blares.

"Okay." I take the box of missing and probably essential espresso machine parts. "I'll deal with this. You deal with the oven—leave the muffins out, and I'll fill the case once they're cool. Then you can go check on Cedella." I'll try to figure the machine out while he's upstairs and out of my hair.

"*Perfetto.*" Mr. Rossi salutes me and scurries off, leaving me grinning. Sometimes my boss just needs to be told what to do.

"Tell her I'll be making the apricot and cream cheese scones! They're her favorite," I call after him.

"*Sei un angelo!*" *You're an angel!*

"Too bad I'm not an engineer," I mutter to the box of missing parts in my hand before setting it aside. Maybe the bad weather will make the morning rush light, and I'll have time to figure out the glossy monstrosity on the countertop.

∾

WITH SNOW MIXED with sleet spitting from the clouds outside, I expected fewer morning customers, but the popularity of my muffins proves me wrong.

The lemon poppy seed ones run out first, like they always do, followed by the cinnamon buns.

Mr. Rossi returns and helps at the counter while I whip up a big batch of Mrs. Rossi's favorite scones, and do a quick check in case there's an espresso machine instruction manual lying around that Mr. Rossi forgot about.

So far, the coffee shop gods have smiled on us and everyone ordered their usual—a drip coffee and a muffin. But in between customers, Mr. Rossi reminds me that "We are going to be on the map! We will be printing money!" so he's probably not going to give up on the machine any time soon. That means I need to become a barista, stat.

In my search, I unearth an old Italian cookbook, and tuck it under my arm to take out front and read between customers. Mr. Rossi pretty much lets me bake whatever I want, and I've been wanting to try some new recipes. Why not biscotti to go with the espresso?

When the morning rush is over, I make a cup of mint tea and hand it to Mr. Rossi. "Why don't you bring that up to the missus?"

"Oh, she'll love that. Thank you, Leah." He beams and disappears, leaving me in an empty shop. I putter around and tidy up, savoring the quiet.

The bakery is my favorite place in the world, but I especially love it before opening, or in the break between the morning and lunch time rushes. That's when I get a chance to bake.

Other than that, I wouldn't change anything about the bakery—except maybe the tip jar with the handmade label taped to it. Last summer, Mr. Rossi scrawled *Leah's College Fund* on it. Totally embarrassing when my fellow high school students were coming in for their morning coffee, especially my cheating ex and his new, beautiful, blonde and scrawny prom queen of a girlfriend. Now that it's February and they're back at their fancy Ivy league college, I can breathe a little easier.

I like my little life. I wouldn't change anything—except

the lack of funds in my or Mr. Rossi's bank account. And getting better medicine for Mrs. Rossi.

I'm in the back, sifting confectioner's sugar to make a quick almond-flavored glaze for the cooling scones, when the bell jingles.

"Coming," I call. My grip on the sugar bag slips and a white cloud puffs in my face. I grab a wet cloth and pat my face before rushing out to help the customer.

A tall man in a long, black pea coat is standing in front of the counter, his dark glossy head bent towards me as he regards the chalkboard menu. My steps slow. I have the strangest sensation, like I'm about to step over a threshold to another world. I'm holding my breath.

He raises his head, and my heart trips over itself. Strong jaw, dark olive skin, patrician nose—his face is beautiful, regal, and unapproachable all at the same time.

I take a step forward and my elbow knocks over a stack of the paper to-go cups. I fumble to catch them, but only manage to kick them, sending them rolling across the floor. Now I'm bobbing and weaving up and down, trying to catch them all.

Is it too much to hope the handsome customer didn't notice? I look up and he's leaning over the counter, his dark eyes on me. His beautiful lips twitch. "Need help?"

Lordy, his voice is as beautiful as his face. Smooth and deep. Delicious.

"I'm all right," I say. Reaching up, I try to set a stack of cups back on the counter, but miss it entirely and they all fall back down. One bonks me on the head.

"Never mind," I say, rising and taking my place behind the register. I heroically ignore the fallen cups littering the floor at my feet. "What can I get you?" I dust my hands off briskly. Calm, professional. That's the ticket.

"*Un espresso,*" he says in a delicious bass that sends goosebumps flowing up my arms. My very floury arms. Crap, I'm covered in flour. And powdered sugar. And some cinnamon. I surreptitiously try to brush some off, but there are still little white and reddish brown flecks dusting my hands.

"An espresso?" I repeat. "We don't—"

The man's gaze swings to my right, and I turn to follow it to the antique espresso maker sitting on the counter. The machine gleams, silently judging my lack of barista skills. "Oh, right."

The bell rings again and three more guys walk in. They're all wearing dark coats and have the same dark and gorgeous Mediterranean features as the first guy. Are Dolce and Gabbana doing a photoshoot outside?

The four guys look so similar, if they're not brothers, they've got to be cousins. The first one at the counter staring at me is the most beautiful of them all. And he's still got his whole attention on me, looking like he's hungry and I'm a sugar-dusted donut.

My blush starts at my nipples and starts rolling slowly up my cleavage—which is on display. Thanks to the heat of the ovens, I peeled off my sweater and am only wearing a white camisole. And tomorrow's laundry day, so I'm down to my last, most ridiculous lacy bra. Pink, of course. Luckily, the cami is thick enough to conceal everything, but the bright straps are showcased on my shoulders. The blast of cold air that tailed the customers makes my nipples spring to points.

"Right," I say. "I'll just get you that, then..." I turn and knock another cup off the counter. This one I catch and clutch carefully as I walk over to my new nemesis. My expression, mirrored in the polished chrome, is full of dismay. I hope the customer can't see my reflection.

The three domes on top are like miniature replicas of St. Peter's basilica. Ornate and just as intimidating. One dome is labeled: *Cappuccino.*

"A cappuccino?" I ask, reaching for the level hopefully.

"No, *principessa.* Only an espresso."

Rats.

Between customers this morning, Mr. Rossi and I figured out how to turn this thing on. I push a button and jump as steam hisses out. Maybe there is a steamer attachment—good for steaming milk.

"Whoops," I say. "Not that one." I pull out the metal thingy, add the freshly ground beans, and tamp them down. I wedge the metal thingy holding the espresso grounds back in and push a different button. A green light comes on.

Then the entire machine starts shaking like it's going to blast off of the countertop. It's the espresso-making cousin of Howl's Moving Castle.

"We just got this espresso maker," I shout cheerfully over my shoulder. I keep my face calm, as if everything is normal. *Fake it till you make it.*

The men by the door smirk at each other, but the man at the front still hasn't taken his eyes off me. There's a prickle on the back of my neck when I turn.

"Come on, come on," I murmur to the machine. "You can do it."

Just when I've given up hope, there's a hiss, and a squirt of unappetizing brown liquid into the paper cup. It smells sort of coffee-ish.

Thanking the coffee shop gods for their continued good favor, I take the paper cup back to the customer and set it in front of him. The four men in front of the counter regard it.

"I'm more of a tea person, really," I say to fill the silence. My blush has reached the crests of my cheeks and is the process of unfurling like twin red flags in front of a bull.

The beautiful man says nothing but picks up the cup and, with more bravery than I've seen in a long time, tosses it back. The room is still as he slowly sets the cup back down.

"It's good," he lies through his teeth.

I wrinkle my nose at him.

"Looks like brown water," one of his friends jokes, and something in the man's dark brown eyes goes icy. From nice and amiable to full of cold anger. His jaw clenches. "Out," he orders without turning.

To my surprise, the men on either side of him—his brothers or cousins or whatever—straighten, and march out the door. The bell jingles in their wake.

I gulp a breath, meeting the beautiful man's gaze. It's us alone in the room. Just me, and the man I served sad brown water.

"I'm sorry," I say, gesturing to the evil machine. "It's brand new... well, brand new to us. We just got it, and a couple of the pieces fell off." I reach down, grab the box, and show him the contents.

He leans over to study the box of parts. A pause, and he nods. "Right."

To my surprise, he swings off his coat and lays it on the counter. His friends are still waiting outside the door, their backs to the bakery. One blows on his fingers as if to warm them, but they seem content to stand outside the shop. As ordered.

Weird.

The beautiful man has gone to the door and flipped the 'Open' sign to 'Closed.'

"What are you doing?" I squeak.

"Making an espresso," he says, catching my gaze and holding it as he undoes his onyx and silver cufflinks. He sets them down and rolls up the sleeves of his luxurious dress shirt.

Why is he undressing? Not that I'm complaining.

He keeps talking, his smooth voice rich as espresso. Well-made espresso.

"*Mia zia* had a machine like this," he says. "It broke and I fixed it. I'm good at fixing things. It made me her favorite nephew." His right cheek creases for a moment and I catch sight of a dimple. Goodness gracious. Model stunning looks and then a dimple.

I go to fan myself and knock over another paper cup.

"Sorry," I mumble. "Durn things... always in the way."

The beautiful man is behind the counter now. I don't know what's happening, but I do know his dark eyes are the color of bitter chocolate.

"You have sugar..." He holds my eyes as he gestures to my front, and I look down in horror. I've gotten powdered sugar all over my front. My breasts look like the snow-speckled twin peaks of Mount Kilimanjaro.

"Oh!" I try to dust it off and end up smearing sugar everywhere. Now my breasts just look glazed.

The customer tilts his head. He's looking into my eyes, not at my breasts. I'll give him points for that. "Allow me," he mutters, nodding his head towards the espresso maker.

On autopilot, I step out of the way. There's something about him that makes me want to follow his orders. Or maybe I just want to study him from the back.

And what a sexy backside he has. A firm ass in sleek black slacks. There's a hint of expensive cologne swirling around me. Not too much, not unpleasant. I lean in closer before I realize I'm sniffing him.

Luckily, he doesn't notice. He takes the box and approaches the recalcitrant machine. Implements clatter as he starts removing and reattaching random tubes and metal protrusions. I hover at his shoulder, my hands helpless at my sides.

"You don't have to do this," I say. "Your friends are outside..." The three men are standing on the snowy sidewalk, their hands shoved in the pockets of their dark coats. They look bored and cold.

"They'll wait," he says, and bangs on the side of the machine so hard, I jump.

"Easy, *principessa*," he murmurs. *Principessa* means *princess*. I know that much from working here.

What I don't know is why he's calling me 'princess.' Or why my fingers are itching to bury themselves in the stranger's thick, black hair.

"This is Stefanos' territory," he says while he works. "Does he give you any trouble?"

"I don't think so..." Stefanos? Have I heard that name before? "Mr. Rossi owns the building, so there's no landlord."

"Hmm." He pauses in his work to reach into a pocket, and hands me a black business card. "If you have any trouble, you call me."

Okaaay. I study the card. 'Royal Regis' is all it says, along with a single number. A cell number?

"Royal Royal," I say, because *Regis* means something like *royal* in Latin.

"Yes?" His lip crooks upward, giving me a flash of white teeth.

"That's your name?"

"My parents had high hopes." He shrugs. His hair flops in his face and gives him a boyish look. "And you are Leah."

"What?" I say, startled that he knows my name. He must have read it on the damn tip jar. "Um, yes."

"Lovely," he says softly, before returning to work. I blush all over again.

A few minutes later, he's re-arranged the levers and reattached the missing hoses, all while I mostly stood around and ogled his ass.

Then he tugs me in front of him, positioning me at the machine with him at my back. He's big, much bigger than I am. The sleek lines of his suit disguised his broad shoulders, but I feel them as he reaches around me, guiding my hand in the correct pattern. First, we put fresh grounds in the metal thingy and then attach it to the correct spot. His hand is warm on mine. His fresh cologne surrounds me, blending with the scent of the coffee grounds.

"Now, Leah," he orders, and a thrill runs up my spine. His breath warms the back of my neck.

"This button," he instructs, pressing it with me. "And pull this." We pull the lever together. "*E presto...*"

The machine hums—nothing like last time's shuddering dramatics. A rich brown fluid shoots out and fills the cup. It smells divine.

He holds my eyes as he takes the cup and sips. "*Perfetto,*" he pronounces. Still looking right at me, he presses the cup to my lips. "Taste," he orders. My mouth opens. I'm not really a coffee person, but the smooth liquid is dark and sinful on my tongue.

"Oh," I breathe. "That's good."

"*Si.*" We're standing so close together, our faces are inches apart.

"How did you do that?" I whisper like we're trading

secrets.

"I have a way with women," he says. "She's a woman, no?"

"Sure," I agree, because I'd agree with anything he says.

"Beautiful women just need to be touched the right way. And I am an expert." He looks at me through his long black lashes.

Is he flirting? With me?

Naw. "Yes, well, it makes sense," I blurt. "You're very handsome." I clap a hand over my mouth so I stop talking, and back up until I bump into the counter. The rest of the cups fall and bounce off the floor.

Oh well. I'll tell Mr. Rossi to take the cost of the cups out of my pay.

A slow smile spreads across his face. He looks like the devil about to make a deal. "You've got some sugar right there." He points to my cheek. I rub the back of my hand over my cheek. My blush makes my skin hot to the touch, like I have roasting coals in my face.

"Here." He slowly raises a hand and swipes his thumb across my cheek. Holding my gaze, he licks his thumb. "Sweet," he says.

"Thank you," I say. I'm not sure why my brain has completely scampered out the door. *Say something!* "So... your aunt liked espresso?"

"Mmm." He looks amused, like he knows I'm fumbling for something to continue our conversation. "But not for breakfast. She liked tea—like you. Every morning, she'd have a cup, and into it she would dip *un biscotto.* A cookie."

"Biscotti!" I brighten. Cookies, I can talk about. Cookies, I know. "I was going to make a few of those for the espresso. And..." I snatch up the cookbook. "There's another cookie here that looks interesting." I flip through the sauce-spattered pages until I find the right recipe. "Chocolate and hazelnut..."

"*Strazzate,*" he says at the same time as I try to pronounce the Italian word and butcher it.

"*Strazzate,*" I repeat, trying to trill the 'r' and give the word the same melodic lilt that he gave it. "It sounds delicious."

The words catch in my throat as I glance at him. He's leaning over me now, hands planted on the counter top on either side of me, head close to mine. The cookbook is sandwiched between us, pressing against my boobs. "If you make me *strazzate,*" he murmurs into my ear while the hair on my neck rises, "I will marry you."

Oh dear. My hand trembles and there's a loud rip. "Oh dear," I say out loud. I've completely torn the recipe out of the book. RIP, page forty-three. I turn slowly and he moves back to give me space—but not much. "I guess I'll have to make it now." I wave the torn scrap of the recipe between us like a white flag of surrender.

Royal's looking at me like I'm a cookie he wants to take a bite out of. "*Mia zia* told me if I ever found a woman who is beautiful and bakes *strazzate,* I should make her my wife."

I scrunch my nose. "That's not a very high criterion, is it?"

He chuckles. "It is harder to find such a woman than you might think."

"Well, I'm sure you'll find someone," I chirp. "It *is* specific... you could put it on your dating profile."

Royal shakes his head and gently tugs the recipe out of my hand.

"You make these, Leah, I'll make you my wife."

Oh, I do like my name on his tongue.

"Shouldn't be hard," I whisper.

His chuckle is rich and dark. My toes curl.

"It'll be easy. I just need chocolate, almonds..." *his dark head bowed close to mine.*

"Do you have Strega?" he asks softly.

"No, but I could order it..."

"I will have some sent to you." He lifts my hand and presses a kiss to it. "Until tomorrow, *principessa*."

He sweeps out from behind the counter. My legs are so weak, one wobble, and I'd be on the floor with the fallen cups.

On his way out, he pauses to remove something from his sleek black wallet and slot it into the tip jar.

Then he's gone, leaving me to shuffle through the sea of white cups back to the counter.

He left a hundred in the tip jar.

2

The next morning, I blow in with a wintry wind before five a.m. There's a bottle of Strega on the countertop, sitting on the ripped scrap of paper that holds the recipe.

"Mr. Rossi?" I call. "Did you leave this here?"

"No, I thought you left it." He sidles up to Big Bernadette, as I have named the espresso maker, inspired by Royal's *she's a woman, no?* comment. "You got the machine working!"

"Um, sorta." With a lot of help from a gorgeous customer.

"Soon, we will be printing money! And look," he holds up the tip jar, "one hundred seventeen dollars, for your college fund." He beams before disappearing into the back.

"Yay." I pick the scrap of paper up. "*Strazzate.*" I try the word out, mimicking Royal's lilting pronunciation.

If you make me strazzate, Royal said, *I will marry you.*

I drop the card with a shiver. Somehow, Royal got me a bottle of Strega for the authentic recipe. Either that, or little Italian fairies delivered it.

I bet I'll get a Royal visit later today. I could make the cookies... and text him? His card is burning a hole in my pocket, but after the morning rush, I have my college class. If I text him, he'll know when to come.

That's the plan then. I tuck Royal's business card back in my pocket where it will keep my phone company until the appointed time. My heart is skipping as I head back to start on a batch of cinnamon rolls.

Royal

THE LITTLE BAKER rushes around the small space behind the counter, making espresso and filling orders. Every so often, I think she's going to finally look up and see me watching her through the front windows, but she never does. She's totally focused on the customer in front of her, giving them one hundred percent of her generous smile.

"You're watching her again," Enzo mutters at my back. "It's been every week for a year. She doesn't even know it."

"Does the prey know the hunter?" I murmur absently. I didn't expect Leah to recognize me yesterday. It had been a year since I last entered her place of work, after all.

Enzo shakes his head. "Enough already."

When it comes to Leah, I'll never get enough. She got my gift, but she hasn't called or texted. Maybe she's too busy.

Maybe's she's afraid.

Enzo takes my silence to mean he can keep blabbing. "Just ask her out. You know she'll say yes." He lights a cigarette.

My fingers itch for a cigarette of my own, but I've quit. New year, new me. My aunt looked me in the eye as she dealt the cards. *This is the year you claim it all.*

"I don't date."

"Then ask her to fuck." Enzo blows smoke. "No woman's turned you down before." His smirk fades when I turn and he sees my expression. He raises his hands. "No offense."

I turn back to the bakery. Today, Leah looks tired, but she's pointed her megawatt smile towards a customer.

When it comes to Leah, I don't want a date. I don't want a fuck. I want so much more. "This isn't about a fuck," I say. "This is fate."

Enzo rolls his eyes, but he's smart enough not to say anything.

They don't understand, mia zia said. *But you do.* That's why I'm the chosen one.

"Your father won't like it."

I say nothing. My father's likes and dislikes don't matter to me. They haven't for a long time. If *La Famiglia* thinks they can control me through him, they're in for a nasty surprise.

Enzo knows this. He tries again, making a show of looking around. "Stefanos has men close by. You know he knows you're here. He's watching."

"So?"

"This is his territory. He's playing nice, out of respect for your father. But soon, he'll make a move..." Enzo's words fade as I turn back to the bakery again. Leah's forehead is pinched. I'm standing too far away for her to see. Does she know how long I've been watching her? Does she sense it?

It's been a year of watching, waiting, setting up the dominos. Soon, it'll be time to flick one over and let them all fall.

"Are you listening, Royal?" Enzo says. He's my second in command, but he knows nothing of the plans I've made. No one does.

"No," I reply. "But I heard you. Stefanos doesn't like me hanging around."

Enzo puffs his cigarette more rapidly. "He'll make a move."

I shove my hands in my pockets. "Then it's time we make ours."

"Seriously?" Enzo tosses the cigarette into the snow. I'm already striding away.

"Yes. Today," I tell him. By tonight, I'll have everything I want. My kingdom, my throne. But every king needs a queen.

This is the year you claim it all. Starting with her.

∿

LEAH

THIS MORNING IS OFFICIALLY a dumpster fire. Nothing goes right. An oven breaks, a timer doesn't go off and I burn a batch of lemon poppyseed muffins—and of course our best customers are all disappointed that their favorite is out of stock.

The morning rush is more frantic than usual but Mrs. Rossi is doing so poorly, Mr. Rossi has to stay upstairs to help her for half an hour at a time.

Then one of my former friends from high school walks in. I say former because Piper only hung around me because of my popular boyfriend. Until he dumped me.

"Oh, Leah, it's you," she says. Her backpack and sweat-shirt are both branded with a Princeton logo. "I didn't realize you still worked here." She glances at the chalkboard menu. "I'll have a grande Americano."

Wrong bougie coffeeshop. I bite my tongue until it pinches to keep from snapping at her. After she pays, I dump regular coffee into a regular sized cup—we only have one size. Most Americans can't tell a drip coffee from a watered-down espresso.

When I set Piper's order in front of her, she glances up from her phone. "Are you still in touch with Josh?"

"No."

"He's at Empire University now, right?" She shifts her weight, straightening her Princeton backpack.

"I think so." With his new girlfriend.

"K. See ya." Piper takes the cup and trots off. I stomp to the back to take out my frustration on the dirty baking bowls soaking in the sink.

Mr. Rossi pops his head into the bakery. "Doing all right, Leah?"

I swallow a sharp response. It's not Mr. Rossi's fault he's had to help his wife all morning and leave me with the morning rush. Nor is it his fault my ex-friend Piper dropped in and made me feel two inches tall.

"All good here." I force my tone to be light.

"*Sei un angelo.*" The stress falls from Mr. Rossi's voice. It takes a toll on him—his wife's condition. There are dark circles under his eyes but he wears a tired smile. "I haven't forgotten you have class today. Cedella still needs me but I'll be back down soon, okay?"

"Okay." I mash my lips into something that's more smile than frown.

"You making the pink cupcakes?"

"No," I say warily. "Should I?"

"You always make them for Valentine's Day."

Right, it's almost Valentine's Day. The worst holiday ever invented by the American candy and greeting card industry. Last year, my boyfriend dumped me the day before, and stopped by on February fourteenth to pick up coffee for himself and his new girlfriend. "Pink cupcakes. Right. I'll get started on those when I get back, okay?"

"*Va bene,*" Mr. Rossi says distractedly, and ducks out of

the bakery again.

So much for making *strazzate* today. It's not like Royal would be back anyway, even if I called him.

Why would he want to?

Happy endings aren't for a girl like me.

Leah

ON THE WAY back from class, my boots are soggy again. I really need to replace them, but I also have to pay my phone bill and rent. Then I have college tuition, which is way more than a hundred and seventeen dollars a credit.

Why am I even bothering with college? At this point it'll take me seventy-five years to graduate, and several lifetimes to pay off the debt.

When the pale pink store front is in view, I try to shake my sadness. Why am I feeling like this? It's not because I'm single. It's not because I'm working at a bakery. It's because when I add up the pieces of my life, the total sum equals pathetic.

Is this what my life is going to be like?

I'm so caught up in thoughts, I'm almost at the bakery when I realize the Closed sign is flipped and the lights are off, but the door is half cracked.

That's odd. Maybe Mrs. Rossi took a turn for the worse and Mr. Rossi didn't want to have to deal with any customers.

I walk in and carefully close the door behind me so as not to let the heat out. Something crunches under my cheap boots. Glass.

I turn and gasp. The front cases are smashed. Broken glass covers the floor and countertop. Glinting shards coat the remaining cupcakes and muffins. Big Bernadette is lying on her side on the floor, dented. Coffee's pooled on the floor, looking like black blood.

"Mr. Rossi," I cry. There's a faint groan from the kitchen area. I fly over the shattered glass to the back.

Mr. Rossi is crumpled in a corner, surrounded by the pots, pans, and whisks littering the floor. I race through the piles of spilled flour to crouch at his side.

"Leah, he groans. The skin around his eyes is bruised. His cheek is red and swelling. "I tried to call you," he mumbles through swollen lips. "Tell you not to come in."

"Easy." I take his arm gingerly, wincing when he does, and help him sit up. We both stare at the wreckage of the bakery. "What happened?"

"Stefanos came."

"Stefanos? Who is Stefanos?" Where have I heard that name before?

"Said I owed him."

"What? I thought you owned the place."

"Not rent. Protection."

"Protection," I repeat. "From whom?"

"From him. Told him I didn't have the money. They didn't take no for an answer."

"Shhh," I murmur, patting his bruised hand. He winces and I feel like an idiot. "It'll be okay. I'll get you to the hospital and then call the police—"

"No." Mr. Rossi grabs my hand and squeezes, despite his bruises. "No hospital. No police."

"But..."

"No. They're coming back."

A chill spreads through the pit of my stomach. I ignore it and say briskly, "Let's get you up and into a chair. I can get you some ice for your head—"

"No. No time. They know that she's upstairs." She. Mrs. Rossi. Bedridden. This Stefanos guy and his men just trashed the place and beat up Mr. Rossi. *They're coming back.*

Mr. Rossi coughs and clutches my hand harder. "I need a favor."

"Anything."

"Go to the safe." He points to the cupboard tucked behind the washing machine. "Now." He pushes me. "Go."

I resist. "You need a doctor."

"Don't want her to know."

"She's going to find out," I snap. This is a mess. This is a nightmare. "Fine." I rise and go to the cupboard, opening it to the safe. "What now?"

"The combination is June 21st, 1989."

Mr. and Mrs. Rossi's wedding date. I suck in a breath and turn the dial, starting with zero, six...

It clicks open, revealing stacks of cash.

"Take it all." Mr. Rossi's breath whistles a little. Did he break a rib?

"But this is your savings," I cry. "This was for her treatment." There are tears in my eyes. "You can't do this."

"I have to." Mr. Rossi chokes. More blood trickles out of his nose. "Please, Leah," he says. "You must take it to them. And be quick. I wouldn't ask you—"

"No, no, I'll do it." I stuff the money into one of our white paper bakery bags, and tuck it under my coat.

I stop at the sink on my way to the door. I can't just leave Mr. Rossi like this.

"Here." I press the wet tissue to his nose.

He raises a shaking hand to hold it. "Go now, Leah. Do you know the office building on the other side of the fountain?"

"Yes."

"Look for number eighteen-oh-four. That is the office." His eyes are wide, the whites flashing. "Don't linger. Tell them it's for the Rossi account. Tell them it's for Stefanos."

"Stefanos. Got it."

"Leah... I'm sorry." For a moment, he looks ashamed. "I shouldn't ask you—"

"It'll be fine," I lie.

My breaths fog in my face as I stumble out of the bakery. The bell jingles, but the sound is muted against my frantic panting. Mr. Rossi's in there, mopping up his own blood. Can he move? Can he walk? I should go back and help him. Instead, I scurry past the bus stop and cross the road, maneuvering around piles of slush.

There's a twinge in my foot but I don't stop marching. Mr. Rossi mentioned a fountain. It's a ten, fifteen-minute walk.

The temperature is dropping by the minute. The sky is gray, heralding a new round of snowfall. Ice crunches under my feet. My thin coat isn't warm enough. I really need a proper winter coat, but I haven't been able to afford one. At least I have my scarf and my mittens. *And a sack full of cash.*

I hold my arms tight to my sides—so tight, my wimpy biceps are starting to ache. Stupid me didn't even think about putting the sack of cash into my purse. It's too big to stuff into any of my pockets. These leggings are old and worn and comfy but have frozen to my thighs, and the thigh pockets would barely fit a business card. I automatically reach my hand into the pockets of my coat. In the right pocket is my phone and the *strazzate* recipe torn from the cookbook. In the other... Royal's business card.

Stefanos. That's where I've heard that name before. It's the one Royal mentioned. *This is Stefanos' territory.* Stefanos, the guy who just shook Mr. Rossi down. The guy I'm supposed to deliver money to.

Does he give you any trouble? Royal had asked. Did he know something was going to happen? How would he?

I've fingered Royal's card so often, the edge is starting to curl. *If you have any trouble, you call me.* Did he mean a situation like this? Was it a warning?

My phone is dead. That's why I didn't get any of Mr. Rossi's calls. Even if it was working, would I call Royal?

What the heck is going on?

My teeth are chattering, and not just because it's cold. They clack together when I'm nervous, too. When adrenaline's soaring through my veins. At my foster home, the alarm once went off in the middle of the night, and we all stood outside on the sidewalk, waiting for my foster mom to stop the alarm from shrieking. My teeth were chattering then, even though it was the middle of summer.

They're chattering now. My morning coffee and half a burnt muffin slosh in my stomach. The fountain is ahead and beyond it, the office building. It's gray and ugly, built in a bland '70 seventies architecture style. The sort of place frequented by accountants and badly funded software startups. Not the sort of place I'd look to find a thug. *The banality of evil, indeed.*

There's nothing for it. I have to deliver this money. Hopefully Stefanos will accept the payment, no questions asked, and let me get on with my life. Leave Mr. Rossi alone. I can go back and get Mr. Rossi to a doctor. But the money for Mrs. Rossi's treatments, the money I'm carrying, will be gone.

I skid on the ice and nearly fall. The white bag slips out from under my arm. The top flaps open and there's a flash of green. I fall to my knees and snatch it to my chest. *Please, let no one be around.* No one to see me acting like a lunatic crossing the snowy square with a sack full of cash, trying and failing not to act like an anxious druggie rendezvousing with her dealer.

I'm still on my knees, clutching the bag to my chest with both hands, when two shiny leather brogues crunch the snow a few feet ahead of me.

A man's in front of me, his long, dark, wool coat looking blissfully warm. That's the sort of coat I need.

The scent of delicious cologne hits me, and I know who it is before I blink into the frozen wind and look up. "Royal." His name comes out with a puff of smoke.

"Where are you going, little one?"

"It's just an errand," I blurt. "For my boss." My eyes stray beyond Royal's solid form. Are those men in dark coats standing by the door marked *1804*?

Royal turns his dark head to follow my line of sight. His lips press together.

He knows. Somehow, he knows exactly why I'm here and what I'm doing. It's got to be obvious, right? I'm clutching a sack full of money.

There's frost on the edges of my lashes. I get to my feet,

blinking rapidly. "Please. I need to bring this to him."

"Leah—"

"He came to the shop," I blurt.

Royal's eyes are black. "Stefanos."

I nod.

We're not alone anymore—Royal's associates are approaching the fountain. Once again, they're all in black wool coats. They look so similar, from their glossy hair to their red-tinged cheeks and hawk-like noses. Like a line of fashion models, or cousins at a family reunion, lining up for a commemorative photo.

"Leah." Royal calls my attention back to him. He comes towards me, pulling off his expensive-looking black gloves. "I can handle it. Let me handle it." His eyes are back to a soft brown. His voice is pure sin.

He holds out his hand. I automatically start to hand him what I'm holding. Then I remember what it is. The money. *More money than I'll ever have in my life.*

"What?" he asks. His associates or cousins or whatever are watching us. I step a little closer into Royal's sphere, close enough that the heat of him emanates onto my frozen face.

"I don't even know you," I whisper.

"I know," he says. "I'm going to change that." He leans back a little, just enough that I miss the heat of him. He shrugs out of his coat and slings it around my shoulders, tucks it closed. "You shouldn't be out in this snow."

The wind blows harder. The snow's falling in wet clumps, catching on my lashes and melting on my cheeks, leaving my skin bitterly numb.

"What is it you want from me?" I can barely get the words out with my jaw clenched against the cold.

"I want to fix it," he says. *I'm good at fixing things,* he said back in the bakery.

And I don't know what it is: the gentle darkness of his eyes, the way the snowflakes caught on his long lashes, or the way he's standing in shirt sleeves with snow dusting the slopes of his shoulders—*He took off his coat for me. Again*—but I trust him.

I get that sense again, like I'm standing at a precipice, looking down. But instead of dizzy, I feel Royal's presence by my side. And I know he won't let me fall.

Surrounded by that subtle freshwater perfume, I stop thinking. Snow's frosting his black hair. He looks too beautiful to be real. But he is real, and it feels right, totally natural, to raise my hand and hand him the sack of cash.

Royal doesn't blink. He doesn't even look at the bag. In one move, he takes it from me and hands it off to one of his clones. He snaps his fingers. "Take care of it," he orders his associates without taking his eyes off me.

The guys turn as one, and start walking towards office 1804.

"What does that mean?" I ask, staring up at Royal. "What do you mean by *take care of it*?"

"Come," he says, crowding forward. "Let's get you out of the cold."

"You mean get *you* out of the cold," I say, because I'm getting concerned. He's a big strapping man, but surely standing out here in shirtsleeves in a snowstorm is bad for him, unless he has some sort of polar bear DNA.

Royal chuckles. He's walking with me—escorting me, really—with his arm around my waist. We're heading in the opposite direction to his associates, towards a big black Escalade. He opens the back car door and bundles me into his arms, lifting me right off my feet. Inside the car the air is blissfully warm, and I half melt onto the heated leather seats.

The door slams and Royal's scent fills the backseat. His big body crowds into my space. I'm scooting my butt back to make room when something cracks in the distance.

"Oh my god." I flinch, my hands flying to cover my head. I don't live in a great neighborhood and the sound of gunshots is familiar. It's different from the sound of a back-firing car.

Royal's expression changes not a bit. With another *rat-tat-tat* round of bullets sounding off in the general area of office 1804, he shuts the door and nods to the driver—a big guy with a shaved head I didn't even notice before now.

More gunfire pops as the Escalade glides from the curb.

"It's okay, baby." Royal puts his arm around me. "I'll take care of you."

My teeth are chattering again.

"Let's get you out of these." He strips off my mittens and starts rubbing my stiff fingers. "Where's your winter coat?" he chides.

"I don't have one." The car's heat vents are blowing full blast. The warmth makes my skin prickle, as if my body is waking up from being so numb. It hurts. I blink back sudden tears.

"My poor angel," he says. "*Principessa mia*." He tucks my hands against him.

The Escalade has rounded a corner. The snowy square, the fountain, office 1804—they've all disappeared. With every passing second, I'm growing warmer. Relief runs through me.

"What was that back there?" I ask before I can stop myself. "The gunshots."

"Stefanos has owned this territory for a long time,"

Royal answers without blinking. "He won't go down without a fight."

I shrink back on the seat. Why is he telling me this?

"Don't be afraid, princess."

"I should give you your coat back." I start to squirm and shrug out of it but he stops me.

"You're still cold." He tugs the coat back onto my shoulders and tucks me into his side. "You have snow on your cheeks. In your hair." His voice rises and falls, lulling me closer. He brushes his hand over my head, and I can't help but lean into his palm. "Reminds me of sugar." He leans in and his lips brush mine. A jolt runs through me, and then a rush of heat that warms me better than the fancy heated seats.

Now I'm too hot. My heart's beating faster, a flush spreading across my face like I've just been staring into an oven.

"Where are we going?" The driver has us whizzing down a road I don't recognize. The day has turned darker. Heavy gray clouds coat the sky.

"More snow is coming," Royal says, not answering my question. "You shouldn't be out without a winter coat."

The last of the adrenaline leaves my system, and my head droops. Something about his scent and the heat of his body makes me drowsy.

"I need to make sure that you're safe," Royal's murmuring above my head. "We're going to my place."

My eyelids are heavy as I stare ahead. The windshield wipers work overtime, swiping away thick clumps of falling snow.

My head drops to his shoulder, and I wake out of my stupor with a jerk. I almost fell asleep on him. "I'm so sorry. I need to get back to Mr. Rossi."

"I'm sending a doctor to his house."

"Okay," I say, even though I don't believe him. What real doctor would do a house call? "Did... Did Stefanos beat him up?"

"Yes." Royal's face turns to stone. "Or one of his men."

I cuddle closer even though I should be terrified out of my mind. "I don't like this," I whisper.

"I know, *bella*. But you needn't worry. I won't allow any harm to come to you. Let me make sure that you're okay."

"Okay."

His dark eyes crinkle. "Okay," he whispers back.

The sudden switch from cold to hot, the drain of adrenaline, Royal's scent—it all combines, and I fall asleep leaning against his crisp Italian dress shirt.

When I wake, we're in a hilly area outside of town. There are mansions here. A lot of them. Giant mix and match monstrosities built with no rhyme or reason into the side of the hill. We pass a Gothic Tudor style one with massive white marble statues dotting its lawn, then a Victorian style one covered in frantic gingerbread trim.

We leave the McMansions behind and head further up a mountain. Now the snowfall, which had thinned a bit, picks up speed. The driver must feel like he's in a video game of some sort, with distracting white specks flying at his screen.

We turn down a long drive lined with a thick cedar hedge. A private road, but it's better plowed than the public road before it. The SUV rolls between the hedges for what feels like a mile, and then we're turning into a large circular driveway and pulling up in front of a real mansion built of solid brick.

"What is this place?" I breathe.

"This is my home. Come." And he pulls me from the SUV.

3

I must still be in a dream-like state, because Royal guides me from the SUV into the house without me stopping to argue, freak out, or even worry all that much. I'm too in awe of the place, which looks more like a hotel for billionaires than a home—much less a young man like Royal's home. How much do Dolce and Gabbana models make?

To my relief, the first place we enter is the kitchen. It's huge and warm with rich Turkish rugs on the wooden floors. Very fancy. With two ovens, it's bigger than the working space of Mr. Rossi's bakery. The marble-topped island is bigger than my bed.

"This is beautiful," I say.

"I thought you'd like it." Royal's lounging in the doorway, leaning against the frame. He's still in his long-sleeved white shirt, which has dried just fine despite getting snowed on. His dimple is creased, as if he's been smiling from watching me gape at his kitchen.

I shrug out of his coat, fold it, and set it on the island.

Without the warmth and scent of the wool, I feel exposed. Even more unsure of what to do.

"Are you nervous?"

"No," I lie, tangling my fingers together. "I'm wondering what I'm doing here."

"I told you, I want you safe."

The question hovers on my tongue for a moment before I find my bravery and blurt, "How do I know I'm safe with you?"

"Do you believe in fate?" he asks.

I stare at my fingers. I kinda do, but I don't want to admit it. "No."

"Right. You will." He leaves the door frame and walks further into the kitchen. "Would you like something to drink?"

"Sure."

"An espresso, perhaps?" Now I know he is amused by me.

I roll my eyes at him and he chuckles outright. He opens a cabinet, revealing a space-age-looking espresso machine built right into the wall, like a safe.

"*Un latte,* then. I will steam the milk." He lets his finger dance over the buttons, turning the machine on and programming it with practiced ease. "Trust me."

Trust me. For some reason, I do. Not only with coffee drinks.

The machine does its work, and Royal sets the tiny cup and saucer on the island next to me. But he must see my uncertainty because he comes close, crowding into my space. A Royal invasion, but I don't hate it. I'm too busy drinking in his beauty and his scent.

He puts a finger to my lips. For a moment, he just rubs my bottom lip as if fascinated by its smoothness. I feel his touch all the way down to between my legs.

"Would you feel better if I let you call Mr. Rossi?" he murmurs.

"Yes."

He drops his hand. Without moving out of my space, he pulls out his phone and dials a number. He holds it to my ear, holding my gaze as we both listen to it ring.

"Hello?"

Relief trickles down my spine as I recognize my boss's voice. "Mr. Rossi? It's Leah—are you all right?"

"Ah, Leah. Yes. I'm fine. The doctor is here. He stitched me up. Now he's looking at Cedella."

"The doctor came there?" I repeat, because I've never heard of a doctor doing house calls.

"Yes. He check me first. The men are downstairs, cleaning. It is a miracle."

"Men? What men?"

But Mr. Rossi doesn't seem to hear. "Thank you, Leah," he's gushing, "for delivering the money."

Right, the money. Royal's men must have delivered it. *Thank you,* I mouth to Royal. He lifts his chin.

"I must go now," Mr. Rossi says in a distracted rush. "Everything will be fine. Big storm today. We will close the shop until it passes. Ciao!"

"Ciao," I say, but he's already hung up.

"The doctor came to his house," I say, because I can't quite believe it.

"I told you I'd take care of it."

"What is going on?" My call with Mr. Rossi didn't explain anything.

"Stefanos made a move, but I was ready. What I didn't anticipate was him targeting the bakery. I had men watching before today, but I had called them away. I'm sorry, *principessa*. I failed you."

Men watching? "Stefanos made a move?" I repeat.

"He did. But you don't need to worry about him anymore. He won't bother you or anyone ever again."

I stare into Royal's coffee-black eyes. All the pieces are falling into place, and I know more than I want to. "Why are you telling me this?"

"I won't keep anything from you, Leah. Not if you ask me. Not if you really want to know."

I squint at him. It's like he's answering a question, but one I haven't yet thought to ask.

"This is a lot." I raise a hand between us, but he captures it. His fingers are long and so warm.

"I know, Leah. But you can trust me." He brings my hand to his lips and kisses my palm. A simple gesture, but one of the most intimate things anyone's ever done to me. The softness of his lips, the reverence in his eyes... something is happening here. I feel it again in my stomach, the seismic shift of fate.

I swallow. "What happens now?"

"Now, you are safe. We will wait out the storm."

Whether he means the snow storm outside, or some metaphorical mafia war, I don't know.

I'm in over my head. This is nuts, but I don't want to step away from Royal. Ever.

Do you believe in fate?

He touches my face with just the tips of his fingers, and brushes his lips over mine again. A light, feathery kiss. When he draws back, his eyes are twin pools of darkness.

"*Bella,*" he breathes, and kisses me again. "You taste so sweet."

His touch turns my thoughts upside down. His lips are

like a shot of Strega, warming me. I sway on my feet, gasping. *Why would he kiss me? What would he see in me?* I try to turn my head, and his fingers tighten on my chin. "No, open for me." He tilts my head and I let him guide me into a deeper kiss.

My thoughts tumble out of my mind. Who cares why someone as beautiful as this man is kissing little 'ol me? I'm going to enjoy the moment before he changes his mind.

I surge to my tiptoes and kiss him back. My breasts smash against his chest. I'm clumsy but eager, and Royal seems to enjoy it. He steadies me with hands on my hips, then angles his head, guiding the kiss so our mouths slant across each other, allowing his tongue to probe deeper. The move penetrates the very core of me.

When the kiss ends, I'm shaking, and wet. Royal's hair is disheveled—I may have dug my fingers into it in the throes of the kiss, but he's otherwise as put together as usual, while I'm shaky and flushed.

"Wow." My voice is slurred; I sound drunk.

He chuckles and swipes a thumb over my lips. "I want to taste you, princess," he says. "Will you allow me to do that?"

"Yes," I say slowly.

He scoops me up—I love how easily he picks me up— and marches through a vast dining room, into a dark inner room lined with bookshelves and wood paneling, where he sets me down on an overstuffed armchair. Seating himself on the footstool, he draws off my ugly boots.

"Your feet are cold," he tuts. His big hands swallow my foot, massaging, warming. My thoughts roll through a slow lazy loop. I can't believe I'm in a *mansion* with *the most beautiful man I've ever met* and he's giving me a *foot massage*. Is this a dream?

He leans in to kiss me again and I meet his lips eagerly.

His tongue sweeps inside my mouth and my pussy clenches. He's taking more than just a taste.

When he breaks the kiss, we're both panting. "You smell like gingerbread," he murmurs. His knuckles brush the swell of my breasts and my back arches, my body begging for more.

"*Mia zia* made them," he continues, softly swirling his knuckles around my nipple. Even through the fabric of my sweater, the light touch makes me ache. "The cookies of my youth. She kept tubs of them on her stairs, and before guests left, she'd put together a tin to take with them. *Biscotti, caramelle...*"

Visions of cookies dance in my head as Royal pushes up my sweater along with my thin cameo shirt. My pink bralette barely holds back my breasts.

"Yes," he breathes. "I need a taste."

I shiver, and he pauses. "Are you cold?"

I shake my head. I'm not cold. Heat crackles under my skin.

He reaches for a remote beside me and points it at the fireplace in the corner. A click of the button, and the gas-fed flames dance over the white stones.

Royal returns to me, pulling off my top layers to bare my bralette. His hands skim along the sides of my breasts. His thumb circles my nipple and tugs the lace edge of my bralette down. He bends his dark head and his hot breath warms my areola. My head falls back. His tongue flicks my nipple, alternating with his finger too. There's a slight pinch as he sets his teeth around my nipple, and tugs. My whole body is rising and falling, riding the waves of sensation.

His hands find my hips and peel down my black leggings. The move pulls me down with it. My back's on the seat chair, my hair spread out in a dark halo around my face.

When I look down, Royal is kneeling between my legs. His long, elegant fingers tug but my leggings are stuck.

"Do you like these?" he asks.

I shake my head, trying to lift my bottom to help him. Instead of tugging again, he rips the seam. The fabric tears under his hands and he tosses the shreds away. My yoga pants were cheap, but damn. It's the first time I've seen Royal anything but perfectly controlled.

Now my pussy is within his reach, protected only by a pair of panties with pink cupcakes on them. He studies it like I'm an espresso machine he's about to take apart and put back together. Like he's mapping out the ways to make me purr.

He extends a long finger and traces up and down the seam of my pussy. His touch through my panties makes my toes scrunch.

He hooks his fingers in the sides of my panties. A jerk, and he's ripped them, too.

"I'll buy you more," he promises.

I'm too turned on to protest. I've never had a man look at me like this, staring at my pussy with the intensity of a starving man offered a perfect peach.

He swipes his thumb up and down, collecting juices. Tilting his head in that familiar way of his, he sucks my essence off his thumb. Tremors ripple through my tummy.

My head falls back. A flush is already spreading over my chest. I'm pretty sure I just had a mini orgasm. "What are we doing?" I ask the ceiling.

"I want to taste you. And, *cara mia*, I always get my way." He lowers his dark head between my legs. His fingers stroke the sensitive skin above my knee. He turns his head to kiss the faint, shiny stretch marks I've had on my inner thighs since puberty, when I gained my curves. He seems fascinated by every one. His tongue glides up and down my seam, feeling incredible. Wet and wonderful, it's so much better than my fumbling fingers. It circles my clit and goes back to lapping at my folds.

All too soon, my body clenches in on itself. My knees automatically close, but Royal holds them open so he can keep licking—long, insistent swipes that intensify the tremors until they threaten to rip me apart. My thighs strain under his grip. He's holding me down, and it whips my climax to greater heights. My head thrashes back and forth.

Finally, the white hot edge of my orgasm passes. I relax, letting the aftershocks flow through me.

After a few final swipes of his tongue, Royal raises his head. His face is as darkly beautiful as ever. His lips are wet. He licks them.

"I've never done that," I say. It's true. My ex-boyfriend never did that for me. I never orgasmed with him.

Royal sets his palm on my pussy and grinds down gently. His touch grounds me, even as it sparks new arousal that threatens to send me soaring higher.

"This is the beginning," he says.

4

R oyal

"THAT WAS AMAZING," Leah sighs. She's curled in the chair. My own cock is pressed against my slacks, but I force myself to rise and fetch a warm washcloth from the closest bathroom. I return, and press it against her slick and stimulated pussy, cleaning and soothing all at the same time. I have plans for her pussy, and I want to keep it in good working order.

That's how I see the world. Machines that need to be fixed. Pipes and joints and screws that should be fitted together so things can run smoothly.

From the first moment I saw Leah, I knew she could benefit from my care. She's poor, overworked, tired. No hope, and no way out. I can fix all that.

And she will fix me. She is the last piece I need to be complete.

"Tell me about yourself," I order as I clean her.

She blinks at me, her long black lashes framing innocent eyes. "What do you want to know?"

"Everything."

"Why?"

I stroke her cheek. Is it too early to tell her why? This house is now her home. My bed is the only one she'll sleep in. For the rest of her life, she'll be beside me.

Maybe it's too soon to tell her all this.

"Because I want to know," I say. She'll need to get used to my orders sooner rather than later. She's already most of the way there. "But if you're tired of talking, there are other things we can do. More I can show you."

Her eyes drop to the bulge in my pants. She gulps then licks her lips, and I'm tempted to take her again. To teach her all the things I want her to know. All the pleasure she's yet to explore.

"No," she says slowly, reluctantly. "I'll tell you everything."

"Good." I scoop her up and sit back down in the chair with her in my lap. Her lips part but she doesn't protest. There's a cashmere blanket beside the chair. I shake that out and tuck it around her. She looks incredible, her dark skin glowing in the shadows, her curves framed in soft wool.

I wait a beat, in case she finds her voice. But I can only hold back so long before I tell her, "You're so beautiful."

She blinks at me. The firelight gleams in her dark curls.

"Um, thank you." She ducks her head.

She's uncomfortable with compliments. Something for me to work on.

"I guess I should tell you... I have no family. Well, besides the Rossis."

She bites her lip and I stroke her knee, running a finger

over the sliver of skin poking out of the blanket to encourage her to continue. "The couple who owns the *Panetteria*?" I ask.

"Yes. They look after me in their own way."

"Continue."

"My foster family said I could have a job. I was one of several children they took in. It was loud and crowded, and so I got out of the house as much as possible." She hesitates and then says in a rush, as if she wants to get it out quickly, "My father died in an accident when I was little, my mom died of cancer when I turned fifteen."

"I'm sorry, *principessa*." I run a hand over her silky curls. "You've suffered."

"Not that much." She's biting her lip again. I touch her bottom lip the way I did in the kitchen, admiring its smoothness and the way the brown fades to blush pink and back again. She has a little gap between her front teeth. It's absolutely adorable.

"I've had a good life. The Rossis are very kind. They even wanted to take me in, let me live with them once. Only..."

"What is it, pet?"

She squirms in my lap. "Mrs. Rossi is not well, and it's a lot to take care of her. They thought it would be better if I stayed in foster care and stayed in school."

"Is that what you wanted?"

"I want Mrs. Rossi to get better."

Hmm. This is something I might be able to help with. "Do you know her diagnosis?" I make a note to call the doctor later, to confer.

Now there's a little line between her brows. I'd smooth it out like I did her bottom lip, but I don't want to draw attention to her worry. Instead, I wait quietly. It's ecstasy and agony, having her weight in my lap in this quiet, dark room. The firelight plays over her perfect features.

Finally, she says, "She has rheumatoid arthritis. It progressed really fast. When she turned forty-two, she could barely move. She told Mr. Rossi to divorce her but he wouldn't do it." She blows out a breath. "Why am I telling you all of this?"

"Because I asked you. And you wanted to."

She looks around the room as if seeing it for the first time. "You ripped off all my clothes."

I come to my feet, hefting her in my arms. She's all silky brown skin and hair and curves. The perfect armful. "Come." I stride out of the library and up the stairs to my bedroom. I want her to be comfortable, and that means keeping ahead of her nervousness. It's time to show her around her new home.

Leah

. . .

ROYAL CARRIES me up a grand staircase. I'm wearing a blanket and a bralette and nothing else. He ripped up the rest of what I was wearing. I'm going to have to deal with that at some point. Later.

I'm still a little floaty. Orgasm endorphins.

Royal climbs the stairs, and we pass a crystal and gold chandelier that's big as a car. "Is it just you who lives here?"

"The staff are off for the day." He carries me down a long hall decorated with gilt-framed paintings that look like they belong in an art museum. When we reach the end, he steps through double doors into a dark bedroom suite that's five times the size of my tiny apartment. "Do you want to wash up? I can draw you a bath." He sets me down but stays close, which is good because I'm unsteady on my feet.

"Or you can just let me go home. If I can charge my phone, I can call a ride."

Royal's eyes narrow. He heads to the window and twitches aside the thick, velvet curtain. The air beyond the glass is a wall of bluish white.

"We're snowed in. My driver is off for the rest of the day, but we should get a plow soon."

"Snowed in?"

"Mmmhmmm."

I narrow my eyes at him. "You planned this."

His cheek curves. "You can teach me how to make *strazzate*."

He lets the curtain fall and his form is draped in darkness once again.

"Here." He takes a limp garment and holds it up. It's a brocade dressing gown, Royal-sized. "You can have a bath later."

Royal already cleaned me up, but I take a moment to myself just so I can explore the massive black marble bathroom. There's a huge steam shower that could hold an orgy. A bathtub made for three—or one long-legged mafioso and a curvy girl like me.

I come out wrapped in his robe, wading through the hem pooling at my feet. I've knotted the sash around my waist, and the front falls into a deep V that showcases my cleavage.

Royal freezes at the sight of me, and it takes the edge off my nervousness. I have curves for days, and he seems mesmerized by them.

He beckons and when I come to stand in front of him, he kneels and slides my feet into slippers. Unlike the dressing gown, they're the perfect size for my small feet. Probably from another overnight guest. Royal probably has a different woman in his bed every night.

I'm not going to think too hard about that.

There's a side table against the wall full of framed photos. On the end is one of Royal and a stunning, dark-eyed woman. She's tall and thin with olive skin and sleek brown hair. She and Royal are arm in arm, her in a ball gown, him in a tux. A matching set.

My heart sinks. That's who Royal should be with. Someone beautiful and glamorous, like him.

I put my hand on my soft belly, feeling a little sick.

Royal sees the move and misinterprets it. "Are you hungry?"

"A little."

His dark eyes gleam as he draws me close. "I have a craving," he murmurs in my ear, like it's a secret. "For *un biscotto*." A cookie.

I can do cookies. I take a deep breath. "Then let's go to the kitchen."

Once we're in the kitchen, my instincts take over. Royal

may be king of his territory and castle, but here, I'm in charge.

"I need flour, sugar, baking powder, salt, eggs, butter or oil." I list off items while Royal stands there with an amused expression on his face. He directs me to the pantry and fetches the items I point to. "Do you have a sifter?"

"I have no idea." He watches patiently as I rummage around the cavernous cabinets in his kitchen. Turns out he has everything I need, from a sifter to two entire sets of Le Creuset cookware, one in Cerise, one in Chambray. Seven types of cocoa, and three types of almonds—raw, blanched, and in the shell.

I even find a mini blow torch for caramelizing the tops of creme brûlee, along with a double set of custard ramekins. I file this info away for later baking sessions in Royal's house. Which is ridiculous. There will be no later. This is just some crazy one-night stand. Common for a guy as rich and hot as Royal.

After he gets his fill of me, I'll be right back to my little life. I only wish his wasn't so glamorous in comparison to mine. It'll be hard to go back to my usual shabby surroundings, even if that's where I belong.

"Where's my coat?" I ask briskly. Royal must have put it away while I was drooling over the complete set of All-Clad pots and pans. He disappears into a room off the kitchen, and returns with my thin coat.

"Why do you need this?" he asks. His voice is soft, but there's an edge to it. "Are you cold?"

"No." I dig in my pocket and find the torn scrap of paper I tucked there what feels like a lifetime ago. "I'm making this." I lay the recipe flat on the marble island. "I need Strega."

Royal finds a bottle in a liquor cabinet. When he sets it

down, there's a look on his face that's close to triumph. He's brought two shot glasses and he fills one to the brim.

He sips a little off the top before putting it to my lips. "Taste." The digestive burns down my throat, leaving an herbal taste in my mouth and a glowing warmth in my stomach.

I sputter a little but find the breath to say, "Good."

He shoots the rest of the glass and dips his head to mine. "Just a little taste," he breathes against my lips. This time, I watch his face as he kisses me. His eyes are closed, long lashes fanning over his dark cheeks. His lips are sipping, pulling on mine, persuading them to open. His tongue touches mine. A little jolt of electricity goes through me.

"It's okay, *principessa*." His thumb strokes my cheek, soothing me. "You're such an innocent, little one."

I wrinkle my nose. "I've got you fooled, then."

He chuckles and leans in for another taste, but I stop him with a firm hand. "Not until I'm done baking."

He could easily overpower me, but he lets me push him back. He leans against a cabinet with his arms folded, and watches me. He's lost his cufflinks but he's still in his dress shirt, his sleeves rolled up to reveal his strong forearms. I'm tempted to put him to work chopping almonds or measuring cocoa but he's so pretty standing there.

"So how long have you lived here?" I ask when I've mostly finished making the batter. All that's left is rolling the cookies into shape.

"My father bought this place some time ago. It's close to our territory."

"So you grew up here?"

"I grew up in the Old Country, raised by my aunt. Italian was my first language. You can tell, by the way I talk."

"Not your accent," I say, dividing the dough in half. It's

easier to talk to someone so beautiful when my hands are occupied with my favorite thing. "But yes, from the way you sometimes construct your sentences. And, of course, you speak Italian."

"You recognize the language?"

"Mr. Rossi says things in Italian all the time."

Royal reaches for a newly shaped cookie and I swat his hand. "There's raw egg in the dough."

A smile plays over his lips but he allows me to fend him off. He does move around the island to stand directly behind me. I'm short and petite enough he can rest his arms on the counter on either side of me. Neither his fine black slacks or the voluminous dressing robe I'm wearing disguise the hard probe of his cock.

Is that a rolling pin in your pocket? I'm half tempted to ask, but I keep making cookies. I've made another six *strazzate* when a light finger comes to play with one of the curls at the nape of my neck. I ignore it, and the way his cock is firmly pressed against my bottom. It's almost a game.

"So your father lives here?" I ask.

"No. Not anymore. No one but me." Royal keeps toying with my hair. It feels like he's smoothing out a curl, and letting it spring back into place.

I want to ask more, but his touch is making my hands shake. Under the robe, my bare pussy is dripping. I squeeze my thighs together, but it doesn't help.

The last row of cookies is turning out to be kind of a mess.

"My father didn't approve of me," Royal says out of nowhere.

"Why not?"

"He thought I was weak. Unworthy. He didn't understand the way my mind worked. But *mia zia* saw something in me."

I'm done making the rows of *strazzate*. I dip my fingers in a warm bowl of water, rinsing them.

Royal's warm breath puffs against my nape. "Turns out my father was wrong, and she was right. I'm very close to fulfilling my destiny. I see the pieces of the puzzle, laid out before me." He splays his hands on the counter as if showing me a picture in the sugar-dusted marble. "That's how my mind works. The puzzle is almost complete. I just need one more piece."

Royal's trying to tell me something and I don't know what. I turn, still in the circle of his arms. I'm trapped between the island and his taut frame. "Royal, I don't know what's going on here."

He tilts his head in that assessing way of his. His hair falls into his face, but otherwise he might as well be a statue, carved from marble by a master sculptor. "My aunt was something of a witch. *Una Bennedetta.* Do you know it?"

I shake my head.

"She's gifted a little, in the Sight. The gift of prophecy. She said, 'When you meet a woman who makes *le strazzate di matera* like I do, you must take her and marry her.' You understand?"

Do I understand? The words—sure, I understand. But what he's telling me? Not a clue. "No," I whisper.

"Don't worry. You will." He tugs the lapel of his robe down my shoulder. "You're covered in sugar again."

He dips his head and closes his mouth over my smooth skin, under the pretense of lapping up the sugar. My head falls back, allowing him full access. His tongue seems to have a direct line to my pussy, no matter where it touches. He licks and sucks his way up to my neck, holding me still with his hand around my throat. I've never had a guy take charge of me like Royal. I've also never had a guy so confident in the ins and outs of my body. My ex barely cared if I got off. Royal seems to have made it his mission in life.

My eyes are half closed by the time he raises his head.

"Sweet," he murmurs.

I rise to my tiptoes, drawing his shoulders down so I can kiss him, tasting the powdered sugar on his lips. "So are you."

"Not really. But you are sweet enough for the both of us." His large hand comes to palm my breast. The lights flicker. For a second, I think it's a trick of my mind, another eclectic shock from Royal's touch, but when I blink, the lights are still off. So's the oven.

There's a hum like a room of engines turning on, and the lights switch back on.

"The generators kicked in," Royal says. "Up here, a tree falls on the lines during a deep freeze. We have power to last months."

This house is so extra. A generator and two sets of Le Creuset? I could stay here forever.

Night has darkened the kitchen window. I can barely see beyond a few feet. "Still snowing," I say.

"Yes, it's quite a blizzard. We might be stuck inside for several days."

"What about the Rossis? Do you think they'll be okay?"

"I have men watching the shop. They'll look after the Rossis. I'll have them deliver food, water. A generator to make sure they have power."

"Why do you have men watching the shop?"

"Protection. In case Stefanos' remaining men make a move. It's unlikely, but I'm taking no chances."

I ponder this. "The men who helped clean up the broken glass. They're ones you sent?"

He nods.

"Why are you doing this? Helping us, I mean." It makes sense that he'd want to expand his territory, but all this work to protect a small bakery? Seems like a lot for the purpose of a one-night stand. But... what else could this be?

"I told you I'd fix it." He shrugs with his hands in his pockets. "I'm fixing it. That's what I do. I want to help you."

"Why?"

"It's too soon to tell you that." His beautiful mouth curves. "How about I show you instead?"

And that's how I find myself on my back on the grand dining room table. Royal sits in the fancy chair at the head of the table, looking like the lord of his realm. He's still fully clothed, while I'm in nothing but his robe and my last remaining item of clothing—a flimsy bralette.

He pulls apart the robe I'm wearing. I get the feeling he likes seeing me in his clothes. He plays with my bralette, tugging it down under my breasts. His thumb hits my nipple and sensation detonates between my legs.

"We should watch the cookies," I say softly, even though I don't really care.

"You set a timer," he mutters. With his thumbs, he spreads apart my pussy, staring boldly at it. "Let's see how many times you can come before they're done."

That sounds like a great game.

It's a little weird to be lying on my back on a dining room table, like I'm a meal to be eaten, but when Royal finishes kissing his way up my inner thighs, he gets down to eating my pussy. Feasting, really. Long swipes of his tongue intersperse with hungry nibbles on my pouty lower lips.

I come within a minute, but he doesn't stop.

"Royal." I squirm.

"Again." He presses my legs apart. A jolt goes through me as he holds me down.

"Tell me when you're close," he orders.

"I'm close," I gasp almost immediately. "I need—"

He raises his head. His tongue leaves my clit and as soon as the pressure is gone, my building climax ebbs away. My whole pussy pulses.

"No," I whine.

He was working me up, the bastard.

"I thought you were going to see how many times I can come."

"I've decided on a new game."

I reach for him, and he pushes me back down. His fingers go back to brushing my sensitive spots, so I subside against the polished surface of the dining table.

He plays with my pussy and massages the sensitive area around my rear pucker. I lift my head again when his finger probes too close.

"What are you doing?" I clench my bottom. My anal ring tightens. Royal keeps studying and rubbing my bottom hole.

"How does this feel?" he asks, like a doctor testing reflexes.

It feels amazing. Too amazing, for such a naughty spot. Heat floods my face.

"I'm going to test something," he murmurs. I'm about to grab his head and shove him away when he bows and puts his whole mouth over my labia. His tongue thrusts into my sopping entrance. At the same time, he twists and dips his finger inside my ass. My orgasm rips through me. I plant my feet and shake. A few more licks and he's rearing up over me, ripping open his pants and exposing his huge, gorgeous cock. His hands tug my hips down to meet his. He rubs my slick center over his long length before spearing me.

I arch back, my body bowing on the table. Royal's hand comes down on my breast, and for once, it's rough. He squeezes my breast hard as his cock hits the perfect spot. My orgasm begins again.

Royal's arms are planted on the table, his thrusts pushing me up the polished surface. His hair's fallen in his face, his teeth are bared. He's more ferocious and out of control than I've ever seen him.

At the last, he pulls out of my sopping pussy and grips my hips to hold me close.

His cum spurts onto my soft stomach. I gasp, my body jack-knifing with my final climax. Royal leans over me, holding my gaze as I tremble with aftershocks. His fingers come to my face, tracing my nose, my brows, my cheeks and, finally, rubbing my lower lip. I open my mouth and bite down on his thumb, gently. A shudder runs through him.

He pulls me into his lap. I sprawl against his chest as he dips his fingers in his cum, scooping it up and feeding it to me. I suck the salty fluid from his fingers.

"Good girl," he murmurs, and I press my legs together, ready to orgasm again.

My head is swirling in the clouds. There's a buzzing in the background—a long, low sound like an annoyed hornet. The oven timer.

I jolt. "The cookies!"

Royal closes his arms around me, his chest jerking with laughter.

I smack his arm. "How long has the timer been going off?"

"A while." He holds me close when I would scramble off.

"Relax. After you set the timer, I programmed the oven to turn off."

"They still might be burned. I need to check them."

"Later," he growls, scooping me into his arms. "I'm not finished with you."

5

R oyal carries me up the stairs, back to the bedroom where he sets me on the bed. "Stay."

I follow orders like a good girl, waiting while he disappears into the bathroom. I scoop my boobs back into my bralette and straighten the straps. My soft belly is sticky with Royal's cum. I feel small in this magnificent room, a disheveled doll set in a richly appointed photoshoot spread in a high-end home living magazine.

Royal returns, and his brows knot together at the sight of me. In the aftermath of the orgasms, I'm wobbly, but I slide to my feet, fidgeting with the robe he gave me.

"What?" I ask, bracing myself for him to tell me he's changed his mind and, snow or not, he's ready for me to go.

"Come." He proffers his hand. My foot catches on the fold of the oversized robe and I stumble. Royal's there to catch me with a frown.

"*Spiacente*," he apologizes. "I should dress you in a proper sized robe."

"It's okay. I kind of like it."

We step inside the bathroom, and my eyes widen. In the darkness, candles glow, each one lit, tapers after tapers along the edge of a bathtub filled near to the brim with steaming water. The air is warm with the humidity the bath is giving off, and from the overabundance of glowing candles.

"What is this?" I breathe.

"A bath. I made you dirty, *principessa*. Now I'll make you clean."

He pulls me to the center of the room and then stops, turning to me. He unbuttons his long-sleeved shirt and pulls it off, leaving him in black slacks and an undershirt that bares his biceps. His muscles are hard and sleek, totally droolworthy.

He tosses his dress shirt to the marble floor and I make a little noise.

"You shouldn't throw your clothes aside. They're expensive."

"Mmm," he hums, turning to me with hunger in his dark eyes. He looks like he wants to devour me alive. My face heats up, the steam curling off the water making my skin flushed and warm.

He tugs the robe down my arms and lets it pool at my feet. He fingers the lace of my bralette like he wants to rip it off.

"Don't," I warn. "I like this bralette."

"I'll buy you a new one."

"You already owe me leggings," I scold, and choke on my words when he strips off his undershirt, presenting me with a mouthwatering display of sleek, tan muscles. His skin is a few shades lighter than mine, an olive brown that speaks to his Mediterranean heritage. I tighten my hands to fists before I run my hands all over him. "Never mind," I say. "You don't owe me anything."

"No?" He angles his body, posing a little. Teasing me.

"No." I drag my eyes away from him. "You've already helped a ton. You don't need to buy me anything."

"What if I want to buy you things?"

My reflection in the steamed up mirror has a furrowed brow. *That does not compute.* "Why would you want to do that?"

"I like buying pretty things." He turns me back to him. I'm face to face with the groove between his smooth pecs. My thoughts stutter into nothing.

He thumbs along the lines of my breasts, fingering the lace.

"I like to own them."

He strips me of my last item of clothing, and I let him, holding my arms up obediently.

He bends over me, brushing his lips over the shell of my ear. "I would spend tens of thousands to dress you, just so I could rip those threads from your body." Those whispered words race across my skin, lighting me up from the inside out. My legs are about to give out when his arms close around me. He positions me in front of him, facing the mirror. I let him move me around like I'm a doll, leaning back into his hard body as he lets his hands roam over me. He's still in his slacks, but the expensive fabric does nothing to hide the steel rod of his cock pressing into my bare backside.

Royal's breath warms my neck as he smooths his hands over my hips and soft belly. He cups my breasts and strokes the sensitive sides of my breasts with his thumbs. My curves fill his big palms, a generous handful spilling out of his hold.

He kisses up my neck while I stare at our reflection.

"What are you thinking?" he murmurs.

"I'm curvy," I say.

"You're beautiful." His hand comes to my throat, wrapping around it and turning my head for his kiss. "Open for me, Leah."

And I do. I'll let him do anything he wants to me. If we only have one night together, I'm going to soak up everything I can.

It'll be over all too soon.

Leah

I AWAKEN IN DARKNESS, blinking in the blissful warmth. There's a long, hard body pressed up against me. *Royal.* I'm in his bed. Across the dark room, beyond the window panes, snow falls silently.

Last night, Royal gave me a bath. At my request, he kept

my hair dry, but personally washed me, running a wash-cloth over all my curves. I may have had another mini orgasm or two, just from his thorough washing of my princess parts.

He scooped me from the tub, drying me off with the same thoroughness and intensity he does everything—from fixing espresso machines to giving me orgasms. Then he took me to bed and made it clear how beautiful he thinks I am.

Now I'm in his bed, still drowsy. I twitch in preparation to inch away, and Royal's arm tightens.

"Leah," he murmurs against the back of my neck.

"I wasn't trying to wake you," I whisper. "I should go." A one-night stand only lasts one night. I have no cause to feel disappointed.

"It's snowing. You sleep now." His voice is muffled by my hair.

"What time is it?"

With a soft snarl, he moves, craning around to check the clock. "Six in the morning. February fourteenth."

No wonder I woke up. This is prime baking time.

I push against Royal's hard arm, but it doesn't budge. "I need to get to work."

"The shop is still closed," he says, sounding fully awake now. "Not only because of snow. Your boss is also going to wait until the shop has undergone repairs."

"You talked to him?" After the final round of sexy times, I passed out. Probably only a handful of hours ago.

"My men did."

"He's all right? And Cedella?"

"Both doing fine. We can call them whenever you like."

I lick my lips. Sooner or later, I'm going to need to return home. But maybe I can keep the fantasy a little while longer.

"It's Valentine's Day," I say, even as I let myself relax against Royal.

He nuzzles the back of my neck. "Did you have plans?"

"Not really." I'd be making vanilla cupcakes with strawberry pink frosting, and red velvet cupcakes topped with thick cream cheese frosting.

"No date?"

"Not since my ex dumped me a year ago. The day before Valentine's Day." So he could take the girl he really wanted out on a date. "Since then, I've been alone."

"Not anymore." Royal kisses the back of my neck, his lips soft and sweet. It feels so good, I close my eyes.

"Eventually, I have to go back to my life," I manage in a shaky voice.

"Or... You could stay here with me." He rolls me onto my back and rises over me, a satisfied look on his face. "I have lots to offer... Everything you desire. Stay until I show you it all."

I'm naked and so is he. It's very distracting. "This is ridiculous." My voice comes out a pant.

He's wide awake now. He pushes my legs apart. "You can't leave. We're snowed in." His cock bobs as he looks down at me. "Looks like you'll be here a little while longer."

"I guess." I lick my lips, staring at the dark shape of his cock.

"Come here," he demands, pulling me up with him. I don't even have time to protest before he bundles me into his lap. I look up at him and he kisses me, mouth traveling down my jaw, to my neck. He drags his teeth over my skin, holding me close. It's just the two of us, a sea of blankets, with the snow falling thick and heavy outside.

He tips me back, cradling me in strong arms. My nerves tingle and I tilt my head back, letting him kiss down the line of my shoulder to my breasts. He shifts, laying me down so he can devour my skin, licking over my left breast, pulling my nipple into a tight bud.

"Wait, stop," I say as his hand skims down between my thighs. He pauses and his gaze travels up my body, his eyes intense as he looks at me.

"What is it?"

My cheeks are flushing as I say it, but the words spill out of me. "I want to watch you make yourself feel good," I say.

He makes an amused noise. "*Si*?" He adjusts me in his lap. "Is that what you want?"

I nod and slide off of him, slipping back into the pillows, propping myself up. He presents me with his palm.

"Lick," he commands, and I do. I lap at his hand, painting his skin with my saliva. "Good girl." He takes his cock in hand. It's rock-hard and waiting, the tip flushed as red as my cheeks.

"After this, we do what I want," he says, "since I'm giving you a show."

My mouth goes dry and I nod. Anything, to see him touch himself, show me exactly how he likes it.

"Do you know how long I've thought of this?" he asks me as he grips his rod, his face turning dark. His eyes burn over my skin, and I don't want to ask him how long, or why, because I'm too busy drinking in the look of him, spine steel-straight, head slightly bowed, as he works his hand up and down his length.

My lips part as he watches me watching him. This is the most erotic thing I've ever done in my life. The wet sound of his hand over his skin makes my sex throb. My thighs tighten together.

I want him, that, inside of me.

I feel hot all over, and he groans, spreading his knees, bracing a hand next to me on the sheets as he works himself over.

"After this, you're gonna give me what I want." His words are breathy and thick. His eyes close tight and his hand stills on his cock, his hips hitching like he wants to fuck into his fist. "Lie back, beautiful."

I obey, flattening myself. He straddles me, his heavy thighs bracing on either side of my body. His cock bobs in front of my face and my mouth opens automatically.

"Is this what you want?" His voice is a soft rasp. "I just bathed you last night. Made you clean. And now you want to be dirty again?"

I'm too overcome to do more than whimper. My breasts are heaving.

He's stroking himself faster now, tipping back his head, caught in his own passion. "Leah," he breathes, and comes. The blast of seed spills from the head of his cock over my lush breasts, frosting my skin with silver.

He leans down, swipes his finger across my coated breasts, and feeds his cum to me. I round my lips and suck hard, pulling on his digit. His gaze goes black.

"*Principessa mia.*" He breathes the words like they're a prayer, and bends over to open a drawer, pulling out two black, silk lengths of fabric. He gives me a look that should strike fear right into my heart. But it doesn't.

"Now," he says. "We do what I want."

I hold my breath as he takes my ankles and ties them apart. Then he settles between my bound legs, and licks me until I beg him to stop.

∼

LEAH

THE SHEETS RUSTLE as I wake up, melting from the dark back into consciousness. My fingers slip along the crisp linen, seeking the warmth I'm starting to get used to finding—

Nothing. My hand closes on empty space and I sit up, my curls tumbling away from my face.

Royal's gone, and my heart squeezes hot and tight in my chest. Light is sliding through the room, gray and overcast. I guess the storm is still haunting us, keeping me here.

The clock on the bedside table has its hour hand pointed to two, and I squeak. *Two in the afternoon?* I haven't slept this late in years.

I need to get up.

The carpet is plush against my feet as I get out of bed, and for a moment I want to leave the blankets rumpled in memorial to an epic night and early morning, but I can't. I smooth the duvet, and straighten the pillows. It seems like a crime to leave things a mess when this bedroom is more beautiful than anything I've seen on HGTV or pinned on my Pinterest board.

Warmth radiates up from the floor, caressing my skin, and I'm very aware that I'm not wearing anything. Me, naked, my curves bare in this beautiful, minimalist shrine to masculinity. Anyone could walk in right now. I sneak across the room, feeling like an intruder in this place, Royal's home.

I squint at the closet doors, wondering if there's something behind them that would work for me. Even a shirt of Royal's would fall down past my thighs. That would be okay to tide me over. It's going to be awkward to figure out what to wear home. *Um, Royal, can you buy me some clothes so I can ride the bus?*

Talk about a walk of shame.

I wrap my hands around the dark onyx door handles, and pull them open.

Lights flare to life in front of me. What I thought was a simple closet is nearly fifteen feet deep and ten across. That's not even the real surprise.

My lips part in shock, and my breath falters to a stop in my throat. This closet doesn't hold a single shred of men's clothing.

Racks line one side, with dresses hung carefully on white velvet hangers. Gentle pink tulle, cream silks, gemstone velvets, all organized neatly in length and a rainbow of colors. I step in and lift one hand, fingers shaking as I carefully flip a tag that's pinned to a spaghetti strap.

Oscar De La Renta, it reads, and I drop it like it's hot. I reach for the next dress, and can't contain my gasp. *Dolce & Gabbana*. I flick through labels. *The Row, Valentino, Zimmerman—*

The blood is rushing to my head as I turn. The opposite wall is lined with neat shelves, rows of softly folded sweaters in what has to be cashmere in glowing colors, waiting to be slipped on and worn.

Whose closet is this? The picture of the beautiful woman with Royal flashes through my head. Is this her stuff?

The closet door swings shut behind me with a whisper. I whirl, and freeze. Hanging on the back of the door is a huge white monstrosity of tulle and satin. A wedding dress.

What the fuck?

I'm going to vomit all over the plush carpeting. Royal has a fiancée, and she has the nicest closet I've ever seen. Tens of thousands of dollars' worth of never worn clothing, complete with tags.

Hang on. Take a breath. There's a lot of wonderful things Royal has said to me.

There's a lot he's not telling you, too.

I've got to get out of here.

I need something to wear. In a daze, I hold a shirt up to my bare chest. It's my size. Plus sized. Not made to a fit a tall, thin Italian Barbie, but a short, curvy girl like me.

My mouth is full of ash. Royal's girlfriend... fiancée... is my size. *Guess he has a type.*

I reach for a drawer and pull it open, hoping to find something normal, like Target underwear, and instead there's a pile of frothy lace, and what I swear is a tag reading *Agent Provocateur.* Once again, in my size.

My heart-rate is through the ceiling. All those things he said, all the nice things he made me feel... Lies.

Rifling through drawers, I find a bra and underwear that looks normal-ish and not worth a few hundred dollars, and quickly pull on a plain sweater, and jeans. The denim is soft against my fingers, the cut flaring on my curves. When I turn, I catch sight of myself in a floor-length mirror edged with frosting-pink metal flowers blooming along the gilt frame.

Everything fits perfectly. It only twists the knife in further.

This isn't a fairytale. Royal isn't a handsome prince. Even if he did single-handedly double the amount of orgasms I've had in my lifetime—all in one night.

I reach for a pair of winter boots, black leather and exactly my size, and keep them in my hand as I sneak out of the closet and cozy up to the bedroom door. It's cracked open, and when I peek outside, there's no one there. Relief floods me. Getting out of here is the right thing to do. There's a reason Royal wasn't with me when I woke up. This was a one-night stand, and it's time for it to end.

I pad down the hall in socked feet, keeping on the thick carpet so the flooring doesn't creak. I need to get to the kitchen, get my coat. Call a ride—if I can find a charger for my phone. Maybe Royal will be out, and I can do my walk of shame without an audience.

We had a magical night, and now it's over. What did I expect? I never had any luck with men, especially not on Valentine's Day.

I'm halfway down the stairs, clutching my boobs so they don't bounce in this new bra, when I hear low, murmuring voices floating toward me. I hold my breath and creep down the final steps.

A door to my left is pushed open a few inches, and I press myself into the wall, watching the two people inside a bookshelf-lined study.

Royal. And another guy who looks a lot like him. One of the many cousins.

I should keep to the plan and continue sneaking out, but

a glimpse of Royal's beautiful face in profile roots my feet to the rug.

Royal. His face embodies the word, regal and perfect. Just the sight of him makes heat roll through me as I remember all the things he's done to me. All the things he's made me feel. Oh god, I feel like I'm going to throw up again.

"Spit it out, Enzo," Royal commands, and I jump.

The man who must be Enzo stops fiddling with a marble paperweight and puts it back on the desk.

"I know what you're planning," Enzo says. "*La Famiglia* requires you to be married to inherit the throne. Is it really going to be her?"

Those words fall to the floor like billiard balls, heavy and hard, and they stop my heart right in its tracks. A cold flush, descending from my head on down my body, has me nearly shivering. I grit my teeth to keep them from clacking.

So it's true. The small part of me that was hoping he was only storing the wedding dress in his bedroom for a friend, dies. He really does have a fiancée.

Royal sighs, and turns away from Enzo, staring into a crackling fireplace.

"There is no one else," he says. "I can have nobody else." He leans on the mantel. There sits another collection of photos in intricate, polished silver frames. His gaze lingers on one in particular, and my heart stutters its way through a series of painful beats.

Of course. The beautiful woman in the photo. Who else would belong at Royal's side?

A sour taste blooms on my tongue. I'm an idiot. A plaything. Something to keep him occupied while he brooded over his impending marriage to Sophia Loren.

And the way he said it. *I can have nobody else.* He doesn't want anyone but her.

Time for me to go. I tiptoe down the hall to find the kitchen, and the side room with my coat. Forget charging my phone and calling a ride. I've got to get out of here before Royal finds me.

I push my feet into the boots and open the door. The wind lashes me across the face, tugging at my curls and promising a frosty walk. Maybe I can get to a bus stop before I freeze to death. But nothing will warm the frozen place inside of me, the iced-over blood sluggish in my veins.

Tears bite at my lashes, welling up in my eyes. The snow crackles under my feet, the top layer frosty-frozen, and the underneath powdery and slippery.

The driveway hasn't been plowed since the snowfall, but I shove my hands in my pockets. I'll make it out of here on my own two feet, with the battered and tattered threads of my pride wrapped around me like a cape. I'm *not* his plaything. And he can't toy with me, not anymore.

I stride forward and, not twenty feet out, my foot hits something under the snow. I go down flailing, face-planting in the cold fluff. Snow stings my eyes, and frosts my hair. I lie there for a moment, wishing I was anywhere else. Nobody in the history of the world has ever been as pathetic as I am.

"*Principessa?*" That smoothed over, melted-chocolate voice finds me, and before I can roll on my side to give him a wavering middle-finger, Royal's arms are around me.

He picks me up, pulling me out of the snow like I weigh as little as a snowball. I'm too soggy and cold to protest. Much.

"What d-do you th-think you're d-doing?" I try to sound snippy, but my teeth are chattering.

"What did I tell you about that coat?" he murmurs back. He curls me to his chest and despite myself, I melt into him. "I see you found some clothes. You look good," he gives a soft *tsk*, "but it's too cold for you to be out like this."

He strides back the way I came, the snow crunching under his shoes.

My hands ball up into fists, but they lie uselessly in my lap, his arms pinning mine against me so I can't do anything but be carried, like a helpless kitten.

"I'm n-not g-going b-back," I say.

"No?" Royal's chest rumbles with an amused growl, and he carries me up the steps and back into the house. He sets me down in the grand entrance and closes the door. I feel about two feet tall.

"What were you thinking, going out with so few layers on?" He fusses over me, stripping the coat from me despite my struggles. "You could catch a chill. I should turn you over my knee." He takes my hands between his and rubs them, like he did in the SUV. The memory smacks me so hard, I can't catch my breath. "If you wanted to go for a walk with me, you only had to ask."

"I wasn't—I was running away, from you, you and your fiancée," I spit out.

Royal cocks an eyebrow at my words.

"Fiancée?" he repeats, like he doesn't know what I'm talking about.

"I heard you talking to Enzo. He said you needed to marry."

"Ah, yes." Royal straightens, looking down at me from his regal height.

"And I found a closet full of clothes—" I reach for my anger and it's right there. I point a finger at his chest. "Right there in your bedroom. Women's clothes. *Her* clothes. I can't believe you would—"

"Did they fit you?" he interrupts.

"What?" I falter, my finger wilting.

"Did the clothes fit? I specified your size."

I open my mouth but nothing comes out.

"Leah, the clothes are for you." His expression darkens. "Did you think I had them here for another woman?"

"Yes?" The image of the wedding dress blooms big and white in my head. Was it also in my size?

"Oh, *principessa*." He lifts his hand and I flinch, but he simply brushes a gentle finger over my cheek. "You have much to learn."

I swallow several times to find my voice. "For me?" I squeak. All those dresses, the lingerie. "You got them for me?"

"I told you I'd replace what I ripped off you."

He did say that. "I thought you'd get me a gift card."

That indulgent smile is back on his face. He shakes his head slightly.

My brain is short-circuiting. "But that's tens of thousands of dollars' worth of clothes—"

"Nothing less than you deserve." He grips my chin with light fingers and dips his head to my ear. "Shall we have a little fashion show later? You dress up for me. I'll kiss you and tell you how beautiful you look in the clothes I bought you. And then I'll rip them off."

A high-pitched whimper escapes me before I can gulp it back. Royal raises his head, laughing at the expression on my face. *I would spend tens of thousands to dress you,* he told me last night. Was it only last night?

There are too many thoughts swimming in my head. "I don't understand."

"I see I have more explaining to do." The humor leaves his face like it never existed. "You were a busy little baker this morning. Cooking up the wrong ideas. Eavesdropping." He traces the line of my jaw. He's crooning but there's a dangerous glint to his eyes. "I'm going to need to break you of that habit. In my world, it's not safe to listen to the wrong conversations."

I can only stare up at him.

"It's all right. I'll keep you safe. But let me make one thing clear." He dips his head. "I will marry..." His eyes bore into mine, demanding I pay attention to every word he says. "You. You will be my bride."

"Wh-what?" My lips part, but no more words come out. He smoothes a thumb over my lower lip, teasing me. My insides quiver and it has nothing to do with the winter air swirling around us.

"I'll give you everything, *principessa*, everything you want. You will be faithful to me, and bear my children. Is that not what you thought would happen?" He leans down and kisses the shock right out of me, the flare of heat from his lips chasing away the cold. His mouth is heated and heavy on mine. He traces the path his thumb made with his tongue.

I crush myself against his hard chest. My mainframe is crashing and nothing makes sense, but it doesn't matter when Royal kisses me.

I'm up on my tiptoes, asking for more, when he pulls away. His eyes are dark, shadowed, his mouth pulling into a thin and serious line.

"But first," he draws out the words, and my heartstrings along with it, "you need to learn a lesson. My wife will be loyal and faithful, always. Do you understand?"

I blink at him.

"Loyalty means not running. Faithfulness means asking questions and not assuming. There will be punishment for you leaving like that."

"Punishment?"

"Yes. You could have been hurt." He bends down and scoops me into his arms. "When I'm done with you, you will not run again."

Royal carries me to the dark bedroom and sets me down on the bed. He looks me over, like he's checking me for damage, and his lips press together in a thin, unimpressed line. My stomach dips and swoops, hating that I've let him down.

"This looks lovely on you," he comments, fingering the sleeve of my sweater. "Now that you know it is yours, do you like your surprise?" His eyes track over to the closet doors.

"You can't buy me with fancy clothes," I mumble, even though part of me wants to swoon in his arms.

I like to buy pretty things, he told me. *I like to own them.*

Royal tugs off my sweater and boots while I wrestle with my feelings. I could let myself go last night, telling myself it was one night. But now?

"Royal, please." I catch his shoulders as he's unbuttoning my jeans. "This is crazy. We just met. You can't buy me all those things." I can't even discuss the 'you will be my bride' part. It's too nuts.

"No?" He's back to being amused. He finishes pulling off my wet jeans and rubs his warm hands up my freezing legs, which, frankly, is a relief. Once again, I'm cocooned in Royal's dark room and delicious scent, ready to succumb to his demands.

But I can't let go like I did last night. It will mean too much to me. These feelings growing in my chest—they overwhelm me. They make me want to run.

He seems to sense the shift in my emotions, and shakes his head. "You will not," he says, pressing me back to the bed. "I will not allow it."

"What?"

"You think I do not know you, inside and out?" He strokes back my tangle of curls, spreading my hair across the pillow. "You will not run again. I will never do anything less than treasure you, *principessa*. But first..." his voice is deep and smoky, whispering over my skin, "there is punishment for you, for trying to run." He kisses the tender lobe of my ear, licking over it in a way that has me grabbing for the front of his shirt to pull him close.

He rears out of reach. "Lie back."

He waits until I obey, and turns to the bedside table to rummage in a drawer. At the sight of the ties in his hands, my mouth goes dry. My body remembers how he tied me down last night, and is making ready for him. Adrenaline fizzes in my bloodstream. My heartbeat is wild in my chest.

"Give me your wrists." He's got four silk strips of fabric. Two for my wrists, and two for my ankles. He ties me down the way he wishes, and pulls the bra I'm wearing down so the whole thing props up my breasts. I'm still in the plain panties. If he rips these ones off, at least he paid for them.

He paid for a whole closet full of them. I can't think about that.

Royal rises over me, studying me like a king observing his chattel. He skims a finger over my soft belly and cups his hand between my legs. His palm presses into my pussy. "This belongs to me."

Oh. My. God.

"Say it." His eyes are demon dark. He drags his hand over my sex, rubbing lightly. "Tell me, Leah, who this belongs to."

"You?" My voice is a barely a huff.

"Me." A wicked grin tilts his lips. He keeps rubbing me.

"Royal—"

"Shhh, little one. No more talking. Just feel."

My thighs are shaking. His touch is light, too light for me to come. I squirm, wanting more stimulation.

"Be still," he orders, releasing me. I whimper, wanting his touch back.

He leaves me, going to stand in the shadows by the bed. He's fiddling with something on his sleeves—his cufflinks. They clink as he sets them down on the bedside table.

He rolls up his sleeves, his gaze never leaving mine. By the time he's bared his forearms, my chest is heaving like I've run up a flight of stairs.

"Such a good girl," he murmurs. "So obedient."

I don't know why those words thrill me.

"You look so lovely, bound and waiting. I could eat you up."

Oh please, yes.

"But first, you need to be punished for trying to run." He heads to the foot of the bed and settles between my splayed legs. He kisses my shaking knees, clamping his hands on each one to hold me down. I couldn't escape, even if I wanted to. Royal's dark hair tickles the inside of my thighs as he licks up one and then the other, teasing the sensitive flesh. His tongue finds each of my stretch marks and traces them. A lick, a kiss, nothing but worship. My pussy throbs, ready for his mouth.

Hot breath hits the gusset of my panties. "You're not to come, not until I tell you," he says, and before I can even ask a question, or protest, his tongue is on me, licking over the panties. The thin fabric lets me feel everything, while dampening the sensation enough to keep me from coming. I arch my back, pushing myself into his mouth. I grab the ties securing me to the bed, hanging on as waves of ecstasy swamp me, stealing my breath. Royal runs his hands up my thighs, holding me open to him, holding me still for the lashing of his tongue. He's pressing me forward, pushing me toward the edge.

Then he raises his head.

"No!" I was so close. I shut my eyes tight and bury the whine that wants to crawl up the back of my throat. I know he'll show me no mercy, even if I complain.

This is my punishment.

I have to take it.

"Are you going to run away again?" His voice is a soft rumble that rolls right through me. I bite my lip.

"You're not letting me come." I can't help how petulant I sound, and he chuckles.

"No. You don't come until I say so. You don't run unless I tell you to. You *belong* here, to me. It's fate." He hooks the gusset to the side and lowers his mouth to my core again. My whole body lights up. No one manipulates my body this well. Not me. Not my ex. Only Royal.

My pleasure is spiraling out of control. My inner muscles clench on air, on nothing. *I'm so close.*

Right before I go over, he lifts his head, looking up at me from between my trembling thighs.

"Do not," he warns me, and I swallow hard, trying to stop myself from tipping over the edge.

"Please," I beg softly, trying to put all my apology in my voice for running, for even thinking that I could escape him.

He strokes the insides of my thighs, craning his neck to kiss the stretch marks on my soft belly. "You have much to learn, *cara mia*. And I am going to teach you." Now he's risen up to nuzzle at my breasts. "You are going to be my good girl. My wife. All this," he palms my pussy, "belongs to me."

My breath hitches. My eyes flutter.

"Look at me, Leah."

I open my eyes wide, meeting his dark gaze.

"I will never allow you to doubt how beautiful you are. I will spend the rest of my life, every last waking hour, making sure you know that you are a gift to the world."

His palm rocks against my folds, gently rubbing. Destroying all thought.

"You are perfect. And you are mine."

I strain my bonds. I need more.

But he takes his hand away. He stands, his fingers going to the buttons of his shirt. I whimper as the white linen and sleek undershirt fall to the ground. His bare chest is muscled and magnificent. He thumbs open his trousers. His pants and boxer briefs hit the floor. I get a few precious seconds to ogle his perfect body before he's climbing onto the bed, sliding between my legs to drape his heavy form over me.

He kisses me, intense and insistent, tongue demanding access, the faint, earthy taste of myself on his lips. The flavor has my cheeks heated and blushing. His cock is in his hand. He guides it to my sopping center, spreading me open with the head. He drives inside me, and I cry out. His expression is serene as he fucks me hard into the sheets, like he knew this is where'd we be, right now, down to the minute and second.

Like he knew I'd try to run.

And that he'd catch me.

"You think you can run from me? You think I'd just let you go? That's not the type of man I am." He slams his hips into mine, filling me to the brim. "I'm the man who takes what he wants." He grinds against me. "And I want to own you."

Oh. My. God.

"You're perfect for me. I found perfection, *cara*. I'm not giving it up." His breath doesn't even hitch as he speeds up his thrusts. "You're mine, you understand?"

It's too much. I need him, need to come.

"Yes yes yes..." Each word is a pleading whisper and he kisses me, then drags his lips down to my ear, breathing there softly as he moves deep inside me for what feels like forever. I'm a wound harp string, ready to snap.

"You may come—" he says, and something inside me snaps. My body shudders hard through an orgasm. My knees grip his hips, my nails rake his back. He groans a half-second after me, and his hips beat a tattoo against mine as he comes hard inside of me.

My chest is heaving hard enough for the both of us, and I grip the ties binding me to the bed. Why do I feel so safe underneath him? Why does it feel so right?

"Good girl," he murmurs. "You did so well. You're perfect for me." He kisses my brow. My eyes fall closed. I'm tired, and the orgasm worked as a soporific, drugging me. He rises and unties me, returning to rearrange me in the bed.

The sheets and covers are surrounding me in his warmth and the soft scent of his cologne. This is where I belong, right here. I drift. His hands trace my curves, but I'm too tired to feel shy. His thumb strokes my belly. "You can't leave me, Leah. You might be pregnant with my child." His words are calm, but I hear an edge of hesitation in his voice, of anticipation. That rouses me. My brows knot, my sex-wrung brain trying to think, but Royal's right. He didn't use protection.

You will be faithful to me, and bear my children.

"I've been careful with you, but no longer," he says. "I know you're clean."

How does he know that? I feel so fuzzy, I don't even speak the words.

"And I got tested," Royal says. "I'm clean too."

"I don't understand," I mumble.

"You will. I'll make sure of it." He kisses me again, and his murmur follows me into sleep. "My beautiful Leah."

LEAH

. . .

MY HAND FEELS HEAVY. That's the first sensation that enters my sleep-fogged mind. I crack my eyes open. I turn my hand over from where it's resting on the sheets, and light flares into my eyes.

There's a ring on my finger, sparkling in the soft ray of sunlight criss-crossing the bed. My lips part, my breath coming in rapid puffs. The starring gem is a huge princess cut diamond, blinding me when it catches the light. It's set in white gold and surrounded by a whole circle of smaller diamonds, as if one diamond weren't enough. The main rock is big enough to knock someone out if I slapped them, if I was the violent type.

I scramble out of bed. I'm alone again. Royal left me to nap. The clock reads five p.m. Royal is probably working, or buying me more clothes, or announcing our engagement to the world. He probably thought the diamond on my finger gave him the last word.

It's a pretty effective argument. So are the faint red marks on my wrists and ankles and the soreness between my legs.

You belong to me.

I have an insane desire to run down to Royal's kitchen and bake up a storm. I haven't eaten today, right? I haven't felt hungry yet, but my stomach's finally waking up.

Chocolate, that's what I need. Chocolate will make everything better.

I go to the closet and exhale, trying to pick an outfit from the many beautiful clothes. The ring flashes at me every time I move my hand. There's a churning in my stomach, something between excitement and apprehension. Annoyance at how presumptuous he was, to put a ring on me, while I was asleep. Nervousness because I don't know how I'm going to talk my way out of this. A sick feeling, because if I can talk my way out of this, it's going to break my heart.

I rifle through the sweaters, and pick one out that's candy lilac, with rainbow threads dripping down the sleeves. I also grab black yoga pants because if I'm going to tell Royal off for putting a diamond the size of a ping-pong ball on my hand, I need to be ready to rumble.

I burst into Royal's office like a tornado, and he turns in his chair.

His face softens when he sees me, but before he can rise, I point an accusing finger at him.

"You," I say. His eyebrows slide upward and his lips quirk, like he's hiding a grin.

"Me?" He looks around the empty room, his expression playful. I like every side of Royal. Protective Royal. Dangerous Royal. Tender Royal. Sexy as FUCK Royal. Royal in complete control. And this, Playful Royal.

On a lesser man, his smile would be a shit-eating grin. On him, it's just attractive and makes my belly melt.

"Did you think, for a minute, I might want to be awake for the proposal?" I ask, fluttering my hand in the air.

His eyes go soft and warm. "I couldn't risk you running again. There's a tracking device in there."

"Tracking device?" I squeak, when I find my voice.

"Oh yes," he murmurs. "You will not escape me again."

I put a hand to my forehead and the diamond clunks against my brow.

"Leah." He holds out an imperious hand. "Come here."

My legs are moving before I can stop them. I cross the room and he pulls me close.

"Good girl," he breathes, wrapping me in his arms and kissing me. "Happy Valentine's Day." He sinks into a large leather armchair and turns me so I'm sideways in his lap. We both stare down at my ring finger and the diamond winking at us. "I told you you would no longer be alone."

There's an explosion where my brain used to be. "Royal, please. I need answers."

"This is your engagement day, so I will entertain you and your theories."

"I don't have theories, I have questions," I say, my anxious fluttering simmering down somewhat. He's relaxed right now, this quiet time just for the two of us. He's back in his usual outfit of crisp shirt and black slacks. His sleeves are rolled up, showing off his taut forearms. I want to trace my fingers the length of his muscles, ruffle the dark hairs.

"Ask, whatever you want," he says, lifting my hand to his lips. He kisses my palm gently and I yank it away. I will not be distracted. Not right now.

"You say you want to marry me..." I stop because saying the word out loud is so unbelievable.

"I will marry you."

Okay. I swallow. "As your wife, what will I be expected to do?"

"Bake for me, naked."

I roll my eyes.

"I'm serious, baby. You do whatever you want to do as long as you spend the nights with me," he says, kissing my hand again. "Your nights are mine."

That shoots off distant, muted alarm bells in the back of my head.

What about his days? If he doesn't care about my days, where is he spending *his* days? With beautiful women? My heart already feels like it's going to shatter, and I must have stopped breathing because he takes me by the chin, gentle fingers on my skin.

"Leah?" he asks, concern on his face.

"I'm—" How will I know he's mine? My gaze travels past him to the fireplace mantle, to the collection of heavy, polished silver frames. Right in front is a picture of Royal with the statuesque, dark-eyed beauty. That's the kind of woman he should be with. She's poised and beautiful. There's more than one photo of him and her—some of them in a group, one of her and him alone. In each picture, they look good together. They look like they belong.

When I look back up at Royal, his forehead is furrowed.

"Who is that woman?" I'm bold enough to ask.

"My cousin. Lucrezia."

"Cousin?" Oh. Of course. She looks a lot like Royal and the rest of his cousins. Silly me, spiraling for no reason.

"We call her Lula," he says, affection plain in his voice. "You'll meet her... in about an hour," he says.

"What?" I shoot up off his lap, but he pulls me back.

"I asked her to come. She's my lawyer and I have some business. No, stay," he secures me in his lap, "I need you here."

"For business?" I ask, and squirm when his hand delves between my legs.

His lips find my ear. "Among other things." He's doing that thing again, with the palm of his hand. If I let him, he'll play me like a fiddle for the next thirty minutes, my brains will leak from my head when I come, and I won't get a chance to question him at all.

I push his hand away. "Royal, you've got to stop. I need you to talk to me. This whole Batman schtick only works in movies, the strong 'n silent schtick doesn't work for—"

He leans down and plants his mouth on mine, swallowing my words. My breath ends in a moan. The waking flower of warmth between my thighs has me rocking closer.

It's not fair. He knows exactly how to kiss me to muffle any protest I might have.

"But... Lula... business..."

"She's wonderful, and she's looking forward to meeting you."

"Oh my god, Royal, I can't do this."

"You can. You will. You're strong, Leah. Stronger than you know. Perfect for me." He silences me again with his tongue.

"Cookies," I gasp when I come up for air. "I need to bake something. Now."

"All right, *principessa*," he murmurs against my mouth. "You can bake something. You can do whatever you like, as long as you stay with me."

7

L *eah*

THE FRONT DOOR opens to a chorus of muffled voices. I freeze, then shake my head and finish washing the big mixing bowl I used. The muffins are almost done. They're cranberry and chocolate chip. I love breakfast foods that are secretly dessert.

Royal spent the first half of the baking session lounging in the doorway, watching me with a half-lidded eyes. He looked so smug, I had to ask, "These baking things... did you buy them for me? Like the clothes?"

"Yes."

"It's too much."

He sauntered closer and cupped my face, ignoring the flour puffing around us. "Nothing is enough for my wife."

Then he kissed me and my brain short-circuited. I

managed to order him out of the kitchen to give me a few blissful minutes to myself.

Now I'm about to meet Royal's cousin, and I'm covered in flour. *Oh well.* I might as well embrace who I am. I can't be anyone else.

The voices round the hall and a brunette with sleek, straight hair and wearing a black pantsuit walks in, followed by Royal. I feel short and shabby in my sugar-dusted outfit.

Lula is more beautiful in person, dark and striking like Royal. She could be his sister.

"So you're Leah," she says, looking me up and down. Her expression is inscrutable, and I don't know what she's thinking. "I'm his cousin," she explains, although I'm sure Royal's already told her that I know who she is. "Royal has a lot of cousins." The two of them exchange a look, and I can't tell if there's some secret meaning there, or an old joke.

"Okay," I say, trying not to sound as awkward as I feel.

"It's good to meet you." She sets down her slim leather briefcase. The Prada stamp is visible on the corner of it. That's a five thousand dollar briefcase. My brain blue screens.

Lula is offering me her hand. I grab it, my wet fingers sliding against her perfectly manicured ones.

"Oh sorry, I was just washing up." I get a dish towel and hand it to her. I use too much force and it flies out of my grip and nearly hits her in the face. "Oh my god, I'm sorry!"

"That's okay." Her dark eyes twinkle. "She cooks and cleans?" Lula raises a brow at her cousin.

"Only if she wishes." Royal crosses to my side and takes my left hand. His expression goes scarily blank.

"It's on the windowsill," I blurt. "I didn't want to lose it while washing dishes." The ring probably costs more than a year of Mr. Rossi's rent.

Royal collects the ring and takes my hand to slide it firmly onto my finger. "This stays on your finger," he murmurs. "Understand?"

"Once again, you didn't ask me," I tease, fluttering my fingers. The ring feels right on my hand. It's so pretty. I'm ignoring the little fact that it contains a tracking device —for now.

"Leah," Royal warns. His thumb strokes over my wrist.

"I understand. No more washing dishes. That'll be your job." I bump him with my hip.

"That can be arranged. I'm good at making things clean." *After I make things dirty,* his dark gaze adds.

Behind us, Lula clears her throat. I step back from the cocoon of warmth Royal and I created, my cheeks flushed from our flirting.

Lula holds up her phone. "Hey, cuz, Enzo's trying to reach you."

Royal pulls his own phone out of his pocket. "I'll be right back."

"I'll stay and get to know Leah," Lula says.

Royal runs a finger over my breastbone, swiping up sugar. He holds my gaze as he licks his finger. "Sweet."

I shiver.

"Be good," he warns, and stalks from the kitchen.

"Well, well." Lula fans herself. "That was unexpected." There's a real smile on her face. My heartrate slows. Somewhat. A little bit.

She leans on the marble island. "I've never known him to be so romantic."

"Really?" I wrinkle my nose, even though internally, I'm freaking out. "He's the most romantic guy I know."

"Maybe with you."

I don't know how to handle that, so I grab a drying pan and wipe it down with a dishrag.

"How did you two meet?" Lula asks.

"I served him coffee. Um, a few days ago."

The oven buzzer sounds and I busy myself taking out the trays and setting out the muffins on racks to cool. Lula watches with narrowed eyes. Is she judging me? Or is she just thinking?

I set a muffin on a small plate. The chocolate and dried cranberry mixture turned out well. "Do you want one?"

"Absolutely." She wastes no time tearing off the paper liner and breaking the muffin open, cooing at the delicious steam. "This is amazing. I didn't know Royal had anything other than takeout menus in this kitchen."

"He said he bought the stuff for me." Of course he did. He's not the type to have muffin tins lying around.

"Oh my god, that's good," Lula moans. "No wonder Royal wants to marry you."

"You know about that?"

"It's kind of obvious." She nods to the giant diamond on my finger. "That, and the way he looks at you. I've never seen him like this with anyone."

"Really?" I lean on the island, picking at my own muffin, hungry for nothing but details about Royal. "I'd think women would be all over him."

"They are," Lula says with her mouth full.

She can't seem to eat her muffin fast enough, and that relaxes me even more. I can get along with anyone who likes my food.

"My cousin doesn't pay attention. He doesn't date. He barely notices women." She stabs the air with a manicured finger. "I take that back. There was someone he mentioned. Someone he met at a coffee shop."

"Oh?" I try to keep my voice casual, but the blood is roaring in my ears.

"Yeah. A girl who helped him last year's Valentine's Day. Her boyfriend had just broken up with her but she saw Royal was bleeding and bandaged his hands." Lula tilts her head. "Was that you?"

I lick my lips. Dumped before Valentine's Day? Sounds like me. But wouldn't I remember helping someone like Royal? "I don't know. I don't remember."

"Hmm." Lula pouts at her empty plate and picks at the remaining crumbs. "Must have been some other *panetteria*. Anyway," she dusts off her hands, seemingly unaware of the bomb she's dropped on my head, "I'm glad he found you."

"I don't know what's going on," I blurt. "I just met him a few days ago and now... he says he's going to marry me?"

"I'd believe him." Lula's poking around the kitchen. She opens a tin and fishes out one of the cookies I baked last night. "He's already booked the church."

I crumple a dish towel in my hands. "I'm waiting for him to tell me this is all a misunderstanding."

Lula takes a bite of the cookie. Her lashes flutter rapidly. "Wow, that's good," she mutters. She points the remaining cookie at me. "I wouldn't hold my breath if I were you. Once Royal gets an idea into his head, he doesn't tend to let it go. He's always been like that, ever since he was a child. Drove his father crazy," she adds in a mutter.

"Did you grow up with him?"

"No, we were together a lot when we were young, but then his dad shipped him off to the Old Country. He grew up with my aunt. She raised him. Uncle Vinnie—that's Royal's dad—swore he'd never let Royal run the family, but Auntie B pulls more strings from across the pond than Uncle

Vinnie would like." Lula tilts her head, like she's dispensing a secret. "She doesn't get along with her brother. Between you and me, not many of us are fans of Uncle Vinnie, but he's the boss so we all toe the line. Except for Royal."

"Oh," I murmur, because what else can I say?

Lula crunches on the last of the cookie. "I don't know what he's planning but you're a part of it."

I gulp. I wanted more information, and I got it. But now I'm sorry I did. I expected a sip of water and got a blast from a firehose.

"Doesn't Royal need a woman who's more..." I stop because I don't know what I'm going to say. More suited to the role of his wife? More beautiful or knowledgeable about his life?

"More what?" Lula's eyes soften, but Royal returns, strolling back into the kitchen and standing between us.

"It's time," he says and holds a hand. And even though I have no idea what's going on, what this beautiful man is about or why he's so set on making me his, I walk to him and put my hand in his.

Lula follows us to his office, a quiet smile on her face. Together, their height is intimidating. They're two tall book-ends and I'm the bedraggled kitten between them. *One of these things is not like the others. One of these things doesn't belong.*

Royal settles me in his huge desk chair. He takes my hand, checking for the ring. He runs a thumb over the jewel. "Did you and Lula have a good chat?"

"Yes?"

The two of them chuckle at my hesitation.

"So, Leah, in addition to being Royal's cousin, I'm also the family lawyer." Lula has her briefcase back in hand. She pulls a packet of papers out. "I drew up the papers you requested, we just need to sign them."

"I can go," I say, trying not to look too eager to get out of here, and appear like I'm jumping at reasons to bail.

"*Un momento*, Leah," Royal says. "We will need your witness and signature."

I huff under my breath—*foiled*—and look around the room while he sits and signs paper after paper. There's a thick stack of it, creamy-white and plush. I glance around the room, trying to act casual.

"Leah," Royal calls and pushes it towards me. "Now your signature."

"Do I want to know what I'm signing?" I mutter as I sign and initial the places Lula points out with her blood-red nails.

"My last will and testament," Royal says, off-hand.

"What?" My pen pauses, but I've already signed the last spot. "Am I witness?" I blink at him.

"No. You're my heir."

"What?" I shriek, and the pen drops from my ice-cold fingers. It thumps on the desk-top, and rolls before falling right off of the desk onto the floor.

Lula's already bundled the papers and stacked them neatly—oblivious, or politely ignoring my outburst. I gape at Royal.

"What—"

The study door opens and an older man bursts in. "I see I'm too late to stop this nonsense."

He's shorter, stockier, but his features are similar to Royal's. This is Vinnie, Royal's father. They have the same Roman nose. Vinnie's hair is streaked with gray, and he's got a spare tire he's been working on for a while. He's followed by two men, in long black wool coats, and dark sunglasses.

"Enough of this, Royal," Vinnie says, glancing at me for a moment before his gaze flicks away. Like I'm nothing, and nobody important. I shrink in the big leather chair, feeling even more like a kid playing 'office' in her father's study.

Lula is silent, snapping the papers into her briefcase. *Between you and me, not many of us are fans of Uncle Vinnie, but he's the boss so we all toe the line.*

Crap. This is the boss.

When Vinnie speaks again, and Lula looks at him for the first time, it's clear that not only doesn't she like him... she *loathes* him.

Royal's face has gone blank.

"You were meant for better things than this. The family has a reputation to uphold. You need to marry the daughter of a Don, maybe a Vesuvi or Serpente. One of the ruling families. Not someone like..." He waves a dismissive hand in my direction.

Lula's eyes narrow, her blood-red talons digging into the fine leather of her briefcase handle. I want to tell her not to bother getting mad on my behalf. I'm not worth it.

"Stop talking," Royal murmurs. His voice is low and deceptively soft. He's the type who doesn't get loud when he's furious. He gets quiet. It's the calm before the storm. I can feel it bubbling under the surface. Lula doesn't say anything either, but she's a little more obvious with her expression—a clear look of disdain on her face directed at one and only one human in the room. Together, she and Royal look formidable. Two sleek Doberman pinschers, focused on the kill.

Royal raises a hand.

Royal's father doesn't see the clues. He keeps talking, like he hasn't noticed his son and niece are furious with him. "There are families who would hand you their heirs on a silver platter. What the fuck are you doing with her? She's a nobody."

I flinch like I've been struck with a dagger.

One moment, Royal's leaning back against his desk, his hands gripping the edge, his dark head down. The next, he's exploded into silent motion. He crosses the few steps between them in a blur. His punch comes out of nowhere. His fist thunks into his father's face, and Vinnie flies back into a bookcase.

Books tumble around Vinnie. He grabs the shelves to right himself, groaning. The bodyguards freeze but make no move to defend the older Regis.

Of everyone, Lucrezia looks the least surprised. She examines her nails, casually, sighing the sigh of someone who's witnessed this type of scene before. I half expect her to get out a file to begin shaping one nail casually, maybe into a point. I tremble.

"Enough," Royal growls. He's not even breathing hard, his shoulders straight and spine stiff. "You're speaking of my bride. This was a test. You failed, Vinnie," he says to his father. The older man groans. "You're no longer my father. You rejected me, I reject you. It's that simple." Royal's eyes are hard, and Lula crosses her arms over her chest, staring down at her uncle. She looks completely unimpressed.

Something big is going on here, but I have no idea what it is. I'm grateful I'm not Daddy Regis. Even his bodyguards don't look like they want to come to his side in support.

He must be a *really* big asshole.

"You won't get away with this," Vinnie says, struggling to sit up. One of the bodyguards takes pity, and reaches down to help him up.

"I already have. Your sister sides with me. I have the support of the Old Country. And when I marry Leah tomorrow, I will have fulfilled the conditions of *La Famiglia*." Royal's eyes light up as he glances over to me. I cover my mouth with a hand. My left hand. The ring flashes its light around the room.

A hand comes to rest on my shoulder, and I look up. Lula's leaning over me, gripping my shoulder, her furious gaze glued to Vinnie Regis.

"They'll never accept her," Vinnie spits.

Royal shakes his head. "The crown has passed. The throne is mine."

His father makes a noise of rage in the back of his throat. "This isn't over." He shoots a final glare straight at me.

I flinch.

"Get out," Royal orders, and Vinnie does, followed by his two goons.

We listen to the front door open and close. There's a minor commotion, and Enzo jogs up to the office door, out of breath.

"Sorry boss," Enzo pants. "They took out Jimmy. Knocked him unconscious."

"Fuck." Lula whips her briefcase off Royal's desk. "I've got a med kit in my car."

"Go." Royal waves a hand to them both. "Secure the perimeter."

Lula and Enzo file out.

I bury my face in my hands.

"Leah." Royal's voice is soft. He sinks to his knees in front of me. "I'm sorry you had to see that."

"It's okay," I whisper. I can't deal with what just happened so I ask the first thing that's been bothering me. "You met me a year ago?"

"I didn't think you'd remember."

"I don't. Lula told me. I'm sorry, I was going through a break up and—"

"It's okay, *cara*. You've been through a lot. But you still took the time to help a man who was bleeding."

I take his hand, the one he used to hit his father. The red knuckles spark a memory in me. A wild-haired man in a dark, dusty coat. His face was bruised, his lip puffy and broken. I had thought he was homeless. He did have beautiful dark eyes. Was that Royal?

"I'd just survived an attack. I wasn't fit to be seen. But you saw me." He clasps my hand, turning it over so the diamond winks between us. "And I saw you. I knew the right woman was out there, waiting for me. And then there you were." His whisper is pure sin, silky and intimate. "No one else seemed to notice you. But I did." Like everything he says, this causes seismic shifts inside me. "I would've come to you sooner, but it wasn't safe. Not until I had more of a foothold."

He's talking about gangs and turf wars again, things over my head.

I swallow. "Your father—"

"He's losing power." Royal sounds dismissive.

"He doesn't approve of me."

"He doesn't matter."

"But what he said..." I close my eyes and let the tears fall.

"No, Leah. Do not cry over what he said." Royal braces me in his strong arms, bundling me into his lap. His chair dips as he leans back, holding my head to his chest. My tears spot his white shirt.

"Poor *principessa*. I'll make him pay for what he did to you."

"I'm okay," I sniffle. Royal presents a handkerchief and I

give a half laugh. Trust Royal to be a mix of modern and old world courtesies.

I fix my gaze on his beautiful face while he dries my tears. His warmth and scent anchor me.

"I didn't speak until I was four years old." He tips my face this way and that, examining it for tears. "My father thought I was a failure. He sent me away."

"He was wrong," I say.

"Yes." Royal grips my chin. "He's wrong about most things."

A sigh shudders out of me, and I nod.

"Forget him," Royal orders. "He's nothing. You're everything."

"You just need to marry someone," I say before I can stop myself. He scowls and glances away then shakes his head.

"I want to marry you. At first, I looked for a bride who would know her place beside me. Someone from one of the three other families, someone convenient. But the more I watched you, the more I knew how perfect you would be. I need someone like you at my side." He rubs his thumb up and down my finger gently, cherishing even this small part of me. "When I am with you, I feel it. Fate," he finishes.

I blink at him through wet lashes. "What if I need more than fate?" I ask, but I'm wavering. He's never let me down. Not in the short time I've known him. He's been so fiercely protective of me, of anyone even tangentially related to me.

He treats me like I'm someone special. Even if I have my reservations, I'm not strong enough to give that up.

"Fate brings us together," he says, "you and me? We get to write the rest of it together. Fate leaves the fun parts for us to discover." My heart thumps in my chest and he leans in to kiss me. I let him, and he slowly kisses across my face, brushing away any tears that are left.

"I don't know," I whisper.

"Trust me," he says. I let my eyes fall closed. He wants me to believe that I'm the best choice for him. I can trust him, but can I trust in the truth of us?

I can try. For Royal, I will try.

~

LEAH

THE WEDDING DRESS FITS PERFECTLY.

I can't believe I'm doing this. But Royal asked me to trust him, and now I'm wearing all of the lace that exists in our state, what with the veil, shoes, bralette and garter belt holding up sheer stockings. And then the crowning glory of it all, the dress itself, a bespoke explosion of tulle and satin. I turn and peer at myself in the mirror, a glittering backdrop of expensive shoes and handbags behind me.

I look like a giant cupcake with too much vanilla frosting. I try to pull the veil one way, and then the other. Am I really doing this?

Lula is also here, trying on bridesmaid dresses. Royal has left the house to attend to business.

"Whoa," she says when I emerge from the walk-in closet. The suite two doors down from Royal's master bedroom looks like a bridal shop, and it's been turned into one for our benefit to prep for the wedding tomorrow. "That's... a lot of tulle."

"I know." I wrinkle my nose.

"It's not so bad. You do look beautiful." Speaking of beautiful, Lula is gorgeous, in a trumpet gown that falls to the floor in a deep wine red that suits her coloring. She approaches me and gingerly touches the tulle that's frothing around my knees, adjusting it here and there. "Hmmm," she says gently, before pinching at my veil. "There, now what do you think?" she asks, and we turn to the mirror.

My eyes widen. There's something about the way she's adjusted the fall of the veil, and arranged my train behind me—

I look like a princess. My cheeks flush. I look like a bride. The woman in the mirror doesn't look like the girl with pastry baking dreams. She looks like a goddess.

She looks nothing like me.

"You're good at this," I say to Lula. "If you ever get sick of being a lawyer, you could be a stylist."

Lula laughs. She laughs easily, which is another point in her favor.

"It's easy when the bride's so beautiful," she says, and her words warm my heart. She doesn't have to be nice to me. She doesn't owe me anything, not even kindness. But here we are, the day before I get married, and she's fussing over me like I'm her sister, not a woman she just met who's now her cousin's fiancée.

Uncertainty wells up inside me again. No matter how tight Royal holds me at night, I still feel out of place. A raisin in a chocolate chip cookie. Like one day, Royal will wake up and see the shy, shabby girl he's chosen, and send me back to the bakery where I belong.

I wish I could be more like Lula. Calm, collected Lula.

"Enzo said that Royal has to get married so he can take over the family," I blurt.

Lula tilts her head to the side, studying me. "Yes. That is true. He also used you to force a confrontation with his father."

"What?" I whisper.

Lula circles me, tweaking my voluminous train. "One thing you need to know about Royal. He never does anything that doesn't net him multiple results. Two, three, ten times the returns. That's why the family is so eager to give him what he wants. They will do anything to keep him happy, and you make him happy."

I press a hand to my forehead. The diamond is heavy on my finger.

"I don't know what to do," I whisper.

"Leah, as long as I've known my cousin, I've never known him to be this obsessed with anyone. It'll work out. You'll see." She finishes tweaking my veil and steps back. "I've got to go. Want me to unzip you?"

"Uh, no, I'll wear it a bit longer." Maybe if I wear it, I'll get used to it.

"You sure?" Lula says. "It's bad luck for the groom to see you."

"I don't think anything will derail Royal from making

this wedding happen." I smooth a hand down the beautiful bodice.

Lula's smile is bright enough for the both of us as she goes to unzip her bridesmaid dress. "You're right. He doesn't believe in luck. He believes in fate."

The house is extra quiet when Lula leaves. Standing and staring at myself in a wedding dress is doing nothing for my confidence. The woman glowing under the soft lights of the guest bedroom before a sea of fine dresses looks nothing like me. I should have let Lula unzip me. Then I could get back to the kitchen and procrasti-bake.

Downstairs, a door slams.

I hitch up the tulle and start walking down the stairs, careful not to step on my train. "Royal?"

Downstairs is dark. I descend into shadows, and when I get to the bottom of the steps, I round the railing in the direction of the front door.

Five feet from me is the slumped form of one of Royal's bodyguards, his gun on the ground beside his limp hand. I catch the scent of stale cigarettes.

I whirl. At the back of the walk-in closet in Royal's bedroom is a safe room. He showed it to me just the other morning in a brief tour, telling me to go there if there was ever a problem. Another freaky mafia wife lesson I need to learn.

Two steps up the stairs, I trip on the tulle.

"I don't think so," someone says, and seizes me around the waist. I shriek and drive my elbow backward into a firm belly. The man grunts and then claps a hand over my mouth, a cloth fisted in his fingers. I inhale the fumes, antiseptic and sweet. My head fogs over, my vision clouding, and that's all—

8

My head throbs like someone's driven a nail through my temple. My cheek is pressed to a scratchy surface. Voices murmur over my head. Male voices.

My heart slams in my ribcage, and I jolt awake. I'm still in the wedding dress. The veil has flopped over my face. I brush it aside.

I'm lying on faded green and yellow cushions, on what's got to be the ugliest plaid couch in existence. The room is musty, with dust motes dancing in the dim sunbeams. The walls are fake wood paneling.

"What?" I mumble with a painfully dry mouth.

"She's awake," someone mutters, and stale cigarette smoke wafts over me.

I push myself up and lean back on the couch. A dark figure looms over me.

Vinnie Regis. Royal's dad.

"Where am I?" I mutter.

"Welcome to my humble abode." Vinnie flicks his cigarette, and ash flies onto the matted brown carpet. "Not as nice as Royal's place, is it? Course, his place used to be mine. What sort of son pushes his father out?" Spittle flies out his mouth. He raises a hand to push back his hair. He's holding a gun.

I press myself into the couch.

"Fucker always was a silent freak of a kid, always plotting." Vinnie notices me cowering in a cream puff of a dress. "I don't know what he sees in you." His lip curls. "*La Famiglia* isn't gonna allow their golden prince to marry some nobody. If he goes through with this—" he waves his gun at my poofy white dress, "they'll reject him. I'm doing him a favor, taking you."

I lick my lips. *Stay calm. Stay calm. Channel Lula.* "What are you going to do with me?"

"Keep you a while, teach him a lesson. Make him trade you for the territory he took from Stefanos. Stefanos was cutting me in." Vinnie keeps ranting. His men hover around him, nodding and smirking at me.

I close my eyes. *Do not cry.* I press my thumb against the band of my engagement ring. Royal will come for me.

I just have to hold on until then.

"Can I use the bathroom?" I rasp once Vinnie's stomped out of the room. One of the goons left to watch me shrugs and points out a door in the wood paneled walls.

In the bathroom, I scoop water into my hands and drink my fill. Twitching my skirts away from the filthy tile, I lean over the sink and stare at my reflection. "Think, Leah." A goddess with big brown eyes blinks back at me. She looks calm, in control. Ready to get married.

Royal is going to come for me, and I need to be ready. If I see an opportunity to escape, I need to take it. Maybe I can manufacture a distraction.

I open the medicine cabinet and stare at the contents. I can figure this out.

I keep my head down when I exit the bathroom. Vinnie is back, lighting a new cigarette. I clasp my hands in front of me.

"Can I use your kitchen?"

"For what?" Vinnie blows smoke in my direction.

I shrug. "I'm a baker. I like baking. I want to make cupcakes. I always do that on Valentine's Day, but didn't get to yesterday."

Vinnie's bushy brows rise. I try to look meek and scared. Unassuming. Out of my depth. I don't have to try hard.

"Whatever. Make yourself at home. But don't get any ideas." He motions to one of his men. "Take all the knives outta there."

Vinnie's goon precedes me to the yellow kitchen and yanks open a silverware drawer, pulling out all the knives. My skirts swish over faded linoleum. "Thank you," I murmur, keeping my eyes downcast. I find an apron that's clean besides a few old stains, and put it on over my dress.

In what feels like no time at all, I'm turning off the oven buzzer and pulling out my creations. A few goons have gathered in the living room, drawn by the vanilla scent. I swan over to the dusty dining room table and set down a full plate of pink cupcakes.

"How'd you get them pink?" Vinnie asks, suspicion written on his face.

Blood in the frosting. "I found a little bottle of food coloring. You can have as many as you like," I say. "I already had mine." I point to a demolished pile of crumbs and baking paper. I did pretend to eat a cupcake, so as not to arouse suspicion.

The men fall on them. Even Vinnie eats one. Pink

frosting smears his face. My cupcakes are too good to be ignored.

While the men are eating their fill, I putter around the kitchen for a few minutes, pretending to clean up. Then I take off my apron and visit the downstairs restroom again before sitting on the edge of the ugly couch in the front room, my hands folded in my lap like a good little girl. The wedding dress poofs around me.

Under the mix of cigarette fumes and the pleasant smell of cake, there's a slight stench of rotten eggs starting to build up. It's very faint. No one should notice it, unless they're looking for it.

I watch the cheap clock askew on the wall. The seconds tick by.

It doesn't even take a half hour, like it said on the box. Fifteen minutes in, the first mafioso groans and staggers to the bathroom.

This is the dangerous part. If Vinnie catches on and orders someone to put a bullet in my head for what I've done, it's all over.

But he doesn't. From the moans and groans all over the house, he and his men are making good use of the bathroom. In the closest bathroom there's also some hacking and coughing. The toilet bowl cleanser I dumped in with the bleach in a stopped up tub must have produced some toxic gas.

I need to get out of here, fast.

I stand and step lightly over the creaking floorboards. The front door is wide open like someone rushed inside and forgot to shut it. They were probably trying to make it to a toilet before shitting their bowels out.

I don't have a phone or a car, but I glide out the door and start up the gravel drive towards the road. I make a great target in my white dress. Hopefully all the mafiosos are occupied trying not to die on the toilet. Or the other distractions I've set up will keep them occupied.

Inside the house, people are swearing. Someone in the bathroom upstairs is praying to God, loudly.

I'm a few quick steps down the walk when the fire alarm in the kitchen starts to beep. The mix of oil and crumbs I poured in the toaster oven finally did its job. Smoke's pouring out of the kitchen, which means the bag of flour and sheaf of old newspapers I shoved in the oven are probably about to catch fire.

I pick up my skirts and start to run.

There are shouts behind me. A few shots ring out, and I duck, still rushing away from the house as fast as I can in this huge dress. I guess the laxatives wore off.

Royal's dad is on the front lawn, gun in hand. He tries to take aim even as his face contorts and he folds over his cramping stomach, bending double. He's pretty determined to shoot me, even as he's shitting himself.

I hoist my skirts higher and force myself to pick up speed. I run like the house behind me is on fire.

I'm at the top of the road when a giant booming blast makes me stagger. I get to my feet. Royal's dad is prone on the lawn, still moaning. Still alive.

Flames roar in the space that used to be the house's kitchen. The fire quickly spreads. Thugs pour from the windows and doors onto the lawn, hacking in the thick smoke. Most are bent in half like their colons are still rioting.

A black SUV screeches up to me. Royal jumps out the back, a gun in his hand. "Leah!" His black hair and eyes are wild, but he tucks the gun away as he strides to me.

Then I'm in his arms.

"It's okay," I murmur. "I'm all right. He didn't hurt me."

Royal crushes me to him, burying me in his wool coat. He jerks his head towards the house, and Enzo and the rest of his men head towards it.

"No!" I gasp. "Wait!"

"Shhh, *principessa mia,*" Royal says, trying to bundle me into the car.

"You can't go in there," I shout to Enzo and the rest. "Not yet. I messed with the gas lines."

Enzo and the men stop short.

In the distance, there's a whine of fire engine sirens.

"Come here." Royal scoops me up and sets me in the car. I fight through my crinkling skirt to grab his lapels. "Royal, I'm serious. They can't go near the house."

"They won't, baby. Give me a second." He tears himself away.

I collapse back into the car seat in a pile of white fabric. I did it. I survived.

Outside the car, Royal stands in a knot of his cousins, giving orders. His deep voice rises and falls. The sound is soothing. I could fall asleep, if I weren't so charged with adrenaline.

"*Principessa.*" Royal pushes into the car and pulls me into his arms, easily overcoming the wall of the wedding dress.

I pull my skirts out of the way so they won't catch in the door. "You know, for two hundred yards of tulle, this dress survived pretty well."

Royal cups my face, forcing me to focus. "Leah."

"It's okay." I press myself to him. "I'm okay."

He steals a kiss, murmuring against my lips, "I'll never forgive myself."

"It wasn't your fault. And everything turned out okay."

Enzo appears by the open car door. "Boss, you're not

going to believe this. I had one of our men drive by and get intel. Looks like the firemen found illegal substances in the house. The cops arrived to take everybody in."

I bite my lip. Is it bad I got Royal's dad arrested?

"The guys all had their pants down," Enzo continues. "They ate some bad shit or something. It stunk so bad—"

"What the fuck?" Royal breathes.

Time to come clean. I duck my head and raise my hand, like a kindergartener in class. The men's eyes cut to me.

"I may have found an expired box of off-brand Ex-Lax and made cupcakes with them," I say.

"Fuck me," Enzo says with awe.

"I also, um, put a bag of flour in the oven, and oil in the toaster. And turned them on. Oh, and dumped bleach and ammonia into the bathroom. In addition to, um..." My voice dies to a whisper as Enzo's eyebrows creep upward. Royal's face is scarily blank. "Tampering with the gas line."

Enzo looks too overcome to swear. He opens his mouth, closes it, and crosses himself.

"Let me get this straight," Royal says. "You took down a house full of thugs using nothing but a smoking oven and cupcake mix."

"Excuse me, I bake everything from scratch." I'd never made laxative cupcakes before, but when my ex dumped me, I might have looked up a recipe a time or two.

Royal's brows are two angry slashes in his face. Is he mad at me?

"Tell me the truth, Leah," Royal rumbles. "Did you take out my father and a bunch of his men with homemade cupcakes?"

"No one expects stealth poop muffins," I whisper.

"Fuck me," Enzo says in a tone of awe.

The blaring sirens are coming closer.

"Uh, boss?" Another mafioso hovers behind Enzo. "We should get out of here before the cops widen the net."

"All right." Royal waves a hand. "Move out." He crushes me to his side. His lips burn a kiss to my browline. "I am taking you home."

9

The girl in the mirror is glowing. She looks happy, even when she bites her lip. I'm back in a wedding dress—a different one from yesterday. The last one survived kidnapping and an escape from a gas explosion, but not Royal's passion. In his haste to undress me, not even the veil remained unripped.

"Yoohoo, Leah?" Lula sticks her head into the dressing room. "You ready to get married? I'm supposed to take you to the wedding. Royal has a last minute meeting with the family."

"Oh." A meeting with the family? I'm not sure if that's a good or bad thing.

"How are you doing?" Lula saunters in, looking fabulous in her bridesmaid dress.

"I'm good." I finger the lace of the new wedding dress. An Alonuko original. I have no idea how Royal got it custom made overnight.

"You sure? No lingering effects from yesterday?"

I flush. I am a little sore, but not from being held hostage. Royal was pretty eager to show me how glad he was that I was back safe and sound. And I was just as eager to reciprocate.

But I woke up alone. Royal left a note and a chocolate muffin, but I'd have preferred him.

"I'll take that as a no," Lula says with a grin. "You might be interested to know, I just came from the hospital. Royal's father and the rest of them need counsel." I stiffen, but Lula doesn't notice. She tosses her dark hair over shoulder. "I'm arranging plea bargains for all of them. The firemen and cops didn't like all the drugs they found. They're going to jail for a long time."

I bite my lip. This is good news, but will Royal be happy that I got his dad in trouble?

"We don't even have to bring kidnapping charges unless you really want to," Lula adds gently. "I figured you might want to stay out of it."

"I do," I say quickly.

"Then that's settled. I have to say it's my first time dealing with a situation like this. Typically, when I do hospital visits, my client has been shot, not taken out by a cupcake. But one of the guys is in critical condition. The rest are severely dehydrated."

"They ate a lot of cupcakes."

"Yeah they told me that." She snickers. "I had to fight to keep a straight face. I can't believe your plan worked."

I shrug. "No one suspected a thing. Pink cupcakes are the most innocuous thing on earth."

Lula shakes her head. "I told Royal he'd better watch himself with you."

"I only make laxative cupcakes in extreme situations."

"Good to know. But it might be a while before I eat anything else you bake."

"That's fair."

We share a grin.

"Seriously, Leah, you did good. A whole embarrassing branch of our family was taken out in one go. The three other crime families in Metropolis are watching. We needed a show of strength if we're going to take a seat at the table."

Lula moves to the mirror and straightens her dress, unaware that she's making my head spin.

"Royal's father was the weakest link, but now Royal has proven that he can clean house. And he did it without having to kill his father. What did I tell you?" Lula holds up her manicured fingers. "Royal needed a bride. He needed a reason to get rid of his father. And he wanted you. I told you." She taps her temple. "Royal has a brain like an engineer. He's always tinkering. Always fixing things in his head. His mind works like a clock."

"Right." I blow out a shaky breath.

"All right, let's head out." Lula grabs her Chanel purse and fishes for her keys. "I'm supposed to drive you to the church. Unless you want to blow off my cousin and head to Atlantic City?" Her tone is joking, but there's a serious assessment in her dark eyes.

"No." I smooth my hands down the bodice.

Lula's dark eyes search my face. "I'm serious, Leah. You don't have to marry him, if you don't want to. "

"I do want to." I might not be totally okay with everything in his world, but I want Royal. "But on the way to the church... is it okay if we make one stop?"

THE BAKERY IS a bright spot in the dark strip mall. Someone's replaced the old door and added a fresh coat of paint. The overhead sign is new and bigger, with pink lettering like I always wanted.

"You'll be okay?" Lula calls from her black Beemer. I nod and pick up my skirts, trudging to the new front door. Once inside, I drop my train, unsure of what to do. The place smells like spices—red beans and rice, goat curry. Mrs. Rossi is cooking again.

"Leah!" Mr. Rossi bursts from the back, Mrs. Rossi right behind him. They sandwich me, taking turns giving me hugs. "Look at you!"

"Bellissima!"

"Ms. Rossi," I choke out. "You look great."

"The infusions are helping." She pats my cheek. Her hand is soft, her dark skin glowing. "Your man is a prince."

My throat closes. "Yes, he is."

"And now you are to be married. You make a beautiful bride."

"Thank you." I finger my veil. "Will you walk me down the aisle? Both of you?"

"Oh." Mrs. Rossi is so overcome, she puts a hand to her mouth.

Mr. Rossi puts a gentle arm around her. "We wouldn't miss it, *Mia figlia*." *My daughter*. "We are headed to the church soon. We just put the finishing touches on the cake."

"You made my cake?"

He beckons, and I follow the Rossis to the back. The cake is a tower of white, tall enough to touch the heavens.

In the front room, the bell over the door jingles madly.

"That door should be closed." Mr. Rossi frowns.

I know who's just walked in before his velvety deep voice washes over me. "Mr. Rossi. Mrs. Rossi."

Firm hands grasp my hips.

Royal's found me. Of course he has.

"Call me Cedella." Mrs. Rossi beams.

"Come, my bride." Mr. Rossi puts his arm around his wife and starts steering her away. "We need to get to the church."

"We're right behind you," Royal mutters into my veil. He holds me still until the shop door jingles closed. The Rossis are gone. It's just me and Royal now.

"You came," I say before I turn. He doesn't let me out of his grasp, but lets me face him. Good thing he hangs on because as soon as my eyes hit his, my knees wobble.

"You ran," he counters. His eyes are dark coffee, his beautiful face stern, but his expression softens when he sees my face. He picks me up, poofy satin dress and all, and carries me out to the baking cases. He sets me on the counter next to the espresso machine that started this all. My skirts overflow, but he crushes them down, planting his arms on either side of me and fixing me with a dark stare. "Leah."

"Royal," I say warily.

He tilts his head. "You wanted a coffee before we tie the knot?"

"I needed a moment," I whisper. My vision blurs and I blink a few times. "You fixed the shop. You fixed everything."

He runs a finger over my quivering lip. "Yes. I'd do anything for you."

"Your dad said the family won't like you taking me as a bride."

He shakes his head. "I just met with them. They can't wait to meet you. They approve of you."

"I am pretty badass." My voice wobbles, but the pride on Royal's face steadies me.

Maybe I can do this. Royal hinted at a honeymoon in the Old Country. I do want to meet Royal's aunt. I hope she'll approve of me. Maybe a tin of cookies is all I'll need to buy her love. I'll let Royal make the espresso.

My reflection in the espresso maker shows a bride. She looks calm, but inside, she's quivering.

Maybe that's okay.

"Talk to me, Leah." Royal smooths back my veil.

"You hired the Rossis to make the cake."

His glossy hair falls in his face as he shakes his head. "They wouldn't take payment. Wedding gift."

I stroke his hair out of his face.

"Mr. Rossi wanted to bake in his kitchen one last time."

My blood ices over. "What?" I whisper. Did they have to sell? Is that how they paid for the treatment? But I thought Cedella said Royal paid for it.

"They sold the business. With Cedella's health back, they want to travel more. Retire to Jamaica."

"They found a buyer."

"You could say I made them an offer they couldn't refuse."

"You?"

"This place. It's yours now. Consider it a Valentine's Day gift."

I tilt my eyes up so I don't cry. Once the tears slide back down, I say, "You're so sweet. I didn't get you anything."

"You're giving me everything. The only gift I want is this." He palms my pussy over the dress. "You're gonna come willingly to the church, or do I have to tie you up and carry you?"

I giggle. "I'll come."

"Good. Because if I had to throw you over my shoulder, first you'd be going over my knee."

A tingle runs through me. But I bite my lip.

"What are you thinking, *principessa*?"

"Are you mad about what I did to your father?"

"My father threw me away like trash because I wasn't the son he wanted."

"I hate him," I say with a vehemence that surprises me.

Royal doesn't seem surprised. He looks pleased. "There's some darkness in you, little one. Maybe that's why we fit so well. The bitter and the sweet." He lifts my hand and kisses it. The ring sparkles between us.

"You know," I say. "You never asked me to marry you."

"Do you want me to ask?" He leans forward, crushing my skirts. His lips find my ear. "Do you want me to convince you, *cara?* Because I can be very persuasive."

"No, no," I say, but he's tossing up the hem of my dress. I rock back on the counter, propping myself on my elbows as he reaches under my satin skirts.

"Royal! We need to get to the church."

"*Un momento.*" He squeezes my stocking-clad knee, finding the garter belt strap and snapping it. "First, I want to make you scream."

I collapse back on the counter, knocking over a stack of paper cups. A cloud of white puffs over me—powdered sugar. When I lick my lips, they're sweet.

Royal presses two fingers into my pussy, the heel of his hand grinding against my clit. "Come for me, *cara*. And while you do, say my name. Tell me who owns you."

When I come, it's Royal's name on my lips.

AND THAT'S the story of why my train left a trail of confectioner's sugar as I walked between Mr. and Mrs. Rossi down the church aisle to become Mrs. Royal Regis.

EPILOGUE

R oyal

A SHARP PAIN knifes up my side. My breath wheezes out. Under my jacket, my shirt is growing wet. My boots clunk over the broken black top. I want to stop and sink to the ground.

Got to keep moving.

The thug came out of nowhere, popping into my path and pulling me into a forced embrace. I wrenched myself away, but not before his knife sank into me, a red hot slash burning like wildfire through my core.

I'm bloody and bruised, but I'm in better shape than him. I left him in a dark pile by a dumpster.

The assassination was like everything my father's ever done. Sloppy.

E tu, padre?

The pink door of the bakery glimmers ahead of me, a

mirage in the desert. My left eye is a bit blurry. Probably turning black. I force my feet to trudge on, staggering up the glass-strewn pavement. A pile of newspapers have spilled out of their glass case and turned into a sodden mass of pulp.

This was once a nice area, but crime and gangs have ruined its charm. Sent the townspeople packing. These shop owners pay for protection, but my father gives them nothing.

That's something I'll change.

My father thought he'd end things with a quiet knifing. What sort of man sends assassins to take out his own son?

He thinks he can best me. I'll take his mansion, his territory, and then I'll take his throne. Nothing can stop me. *La Familigia* will back the victor. The wheels and cogs in my head are turning. There's just one missing piece.

The bell over the bakery door rings out, announcing a customer leaving. I stop, leaning against the wall like an addict contemplating his next fix.

A young couple blows out of the bakery. Both are blond and laughing, arm in arm. They look like brother and sister, wearing matching Empire University sweatshirts. I wait for them to jump into their bright red Camaro and drive off before limping to the Panetteria door.

More of my father's assassins might be looking for me and I need a place to hide. They won't expect me to have walked this far on foot. I blink at my boots. Have I left a trail of blood? A knife in the gut will do that.

I push open the bakery door. The bell cha-chings and the sweet scent hits me. For a moment I'm back in *mia zia*'s kitchen, watching her roll out the dough with her floury arms jiggling.

A young woman stands behind the counter. Her eyes are

red rimmed but she gives me a brave smile. "Hello, welcome to *Panetteria Principessa*." She pronounces the Italian perfectly. "What can I help you with?"

I straighten as best I can, limping to inspect the bakery cases. My reflection in the glass shows an unkempt man with sallow cheeks and dark crevices under his eyes. I look twenty years older than I am. I look like a homeless man.

I am a homeless man. For now.

Until I take my father's mansion. That will be my first move.

"*Un caffè, per favore.*" My voice is a guttural rasp.

She bustles to get it. I lean a little too heavily on the counter and when she returns, she nearly drops the cup.

"Oh my god," she says. "You're bleeding."

"It's nothing." I wave a hand and wince. "Do not trouble yourself."

"No, no, wait here." She whirls and heads to the door leading to the back of the shop. Through the haze of pain, I focus on her curvy backside.

The burn in my side fades to nothing. By the time she returns with a first aid kit, I'm standing taller.

"May I?" She gestures to my hand.

At my nod, she lifts it and begins to clean the slash on my palm with gentle hands. Funny, I didn't even feel that wound. The one under my jacket is much greater. What would this little baker do if I shrugged off my layers and showed her my red-stained shirt?

Up close, I can study her snub nose, her dark lashes, her bright doe eyes. She's been crying, but there's more color in her cheeks now than when I first came in.

"Did someone upset you?" I ask as she bandages the cut.

"Oh, it's nothing." She blinks and sniffles. "My boyfriend just broke up with me," she admits. "That was him and his new girlfriend who left just now. They acted like..." Her voice drops to a whisper. "They acted like I was nobody to them. We spent four years together in high school." Her voice wobbles. "Anyway."

She's upset, and still she gives what she can to me. A perfect stranger.

She reaches for a bakery box and sets one perfect, pink-frosted cupcake into it. "Happy Valentine's Day." She hands me the white box. There's the barest quiver in her lower lip. "I hope yours is better than mine."

"Thank you." It's all I can do not to leap over the counter to thank her properly, knife wound be damned.

I stroll to the door, bakery box in hand. I pause with my hand on the door and twist to ask her, "Do you believe in fate?"

Her brow furrows, but she doesn't say no.

A plan is brewing inside me. The puzzle I've been trying to solve, shifting and locking together.

She is the missing piece.

It's too soon to say this. "Something tells me next year's Valentine's Day will be better than this one."

"I hope so," she says.

I dip my head, and wrench the door open, striding into the day. Soon, I will return.

I'm coming for you, principessa.

WANT MORE LEAH & Royal? Read **A Bun In The Oven,** an exclusive extra scene starring Leah & Royal from *Revenge is Sweet*

By Lee Savino

. . .

"CARA," *he groans. "You're perfect for me." Plunging his cock deep inside, the angle is just right, each pass rubbing my G spot. The deep sensation makes my legs quiver. "I'm going to tie you up and leave you at my mercy, and when the time is right,"—he slows his thrusts, rolling his hips so I feel his every inch—"I'm going to breed you."*

* * *

Go here to read it: https://geni.us/Abunintheoven

ALSO BY LEE SAVINO

Want more dark romance? Check out the Innocence Trilogy
written with Stasia Black. Start with Innocence: dark mafia
romance.

Dark Mafia Romance

A Dark Mafia Romance trilogy with Stasia Black
Innocence
Awakening
Queen of the Underworld

Beauty and the Rose trilogy with Stasia Black
Beauty's Beast
Beauty & the Thorns
Beauty & the Rose

Contemporary Romance

Royal Bad Boy
Royally Fake Fiancé
Beauty & The Lumberjacks
Her Marine Daddy
Her Dueling Daddies

~

Paranormal romance

Berserker Saga
Sold to the Berserkers
Mated to the Berserkers
Bred by the Berserkers (FREE novella only available at
www.leesavino.com)
Taken by the Berserkers
Given to the Berserkers
Claimed by the Berserkers
Rescued by the Berserker
Captured by the Berserkers
Kidnapped by the Berserkers
Bonded to the Berserkers
Berserker Babies
Night of the Berserkers
Owned by the Berserkers
Tamed by the Berserkers
Mastered by the Berserkers
Surrendered to the Berserkers

Berserker Warriors
Aegir
Siebold with Ines Johnson

Bad Boy Alphas with Renee Rose
Alpha's Temptation
Alpha's Danger
Alpha's Prize
Alpha's Challenge
Alpha's Obsession

Alpha's Desire
Alpha's War
Alpha's Mission
Alpha's Bane
Alpha's Secret
Alpha's Prey
Alpha's Sun

Shifter Ops with Renee Rose
Alpha's Moon
Alpha's Vow
Alpha's Revenge
Alpha's Fire
Alpha's Rescue
Alpha's Command

Midnight Doms with Renee Rose
Alpha's Blood
His Captive Mortal
All Souls Night

Sci fi romance

Planet of Kings with Tabitha Black
Brutal Mate
Brutal Claim
Brutal Capture
Brutal Beast

Tsenturion Warriors with Golden Angel
Alien Captive

Alien Tribute
Alien Abduction

Dragons in Exile with Lili Zander
Draekon Mate
Draekon Fire
Draekon Heart
Draekon Abduction
Draekon Destiny
Daughter of Draekons
Draekon Fever
Draekon Rogue
Draekon Holiday

Draekon Rebel Force with Lili Zander
Draekon Warrior
Draekon Conqueror
Draekon Pirate
Draekon Warlord
Draekon Guardian

Cowboy Romance

Wild Whip Ranch with Tristan River
Cowboy's Babygirl
Taming His Wild Girl

ABOUT LEE SAVINO

Lee Savino is a USA today bestselling author of smexy romance. Smexy, as in "smart and sexy." Find her in the Goddess Group on facebook and download a free book at www.leesavino.com!